A Girl Like Me

Also by Ni-Ni Simone

Shortie Like Mine

If I Was Your Girl

Published by Dafina Books

A Girl Like Me

Ni-Ni Simone

KENSINGTON PUBLISHING CORP.
http://www.kensingtonbooks.com

DAFINA BOOKS are published by

Kensington Publishing Corp.
850 Third Avenue
New York, NY 10022

All Kensington titles, imprints and distributed lines are available at special quantity discounts for bulk purchases for sales promotion, premiums, fund-raising, educational or institutional use.

Special book excerpts or customized printings can also be created to fit specific needs. For details, write or phone the office of the Kensington Special Sales Manager: Attn. Special Sales Department. Kensington Publishing Corp., 850 Third Avenue, New York, NY 10022. Phone: 1-800-221-2647.

Dafina and the Dafina logo Reg. U.S. Pat. & TM Off.

ISBN-13: 978-0-7582-2843-7
ISBN-10: 0-7582-2843-0

First Printing: December 2008
10 9 8 7 6 5 4 3 2 1

Printed in the United States of America

To my little cousins, Kristen and Korynn,
who respectively grew from Kissi and Chubba
to beautiful young women!

Acknowledgments

To my Lord and Savior Jesus Christ, I thank You for Your grace and mercy and for Your multitude of blessings. I pray to be able to show the world through my writing that You are limitless.

To my parents and my husband for your love and support.

To my Taylor, Sydney, and Zion for bearing with me and my deadlines (LOL).

To everyone who has ever supported me and my career, I thank you for your love, support, and encouragement.

To my editors and publishing families, thanks for your support and for believing in my ability.

To the fans, thanks for continuing to support me. I am forever grateful for people like you!

And to all the little girls who dared to dream, I wrote this one especially for you! Be sure to email me at *nini_simone@yahoo.com*.

Be Blessed,

Ni-Ni Simone!

SPIN IT . . .

Track 1

I used to think I was the only one in the world like me and then I realized that there were a zillion mes . . . this is just my story. And this is how it all started. . . .

I'd prayed for my boyfriend, but after a few years it was time to renegotiate. I wanted a new boo. Scratch that—I needed a new boo . . . and not any ole kinda boo, but a Hot Boy. Pants saggin' and timbs draggin'. A Lil Wayne or a Haneef type boo—one who—

"Elite," my eight-year-old sister, Aniyah, interrupted me as she lifted her head from under the covers. "Can you tell God I want a boo, too? But I want a Patrick from SpongeBob type boo."

And who said I was talking to this chick?

"Patrick?!" Aniyah's fraternal twin, Sydney, butted

in. She peeked her head out from under the covers and said, "He keeps losin' his underwear."

"Well, you shouldn't be lookin'!" Aniyah snapped, getting offended. "You're way too grown!"

Sydney moved her hand midway up her face. "You better talk to the hand, 'cause the face don't understand."

"Oh, you got me twisted!"

"Alright!" I snapped, and they quickly retreated back under the covers.

I just wanted to put you down on this real quick: late at night, when the sun was setting and the moon was just right, I liked to pretend the ghetto twins didn't exist. It was a little difficult, though, considering we not only shared a room, but they also slept at the foot of my bed. Which is why I made them go to sleep at least an hour before me, so I could have time to think. Otherwise, when would I have found time to get my famous boo fantasy on? Crazy, right? But not to me. That's why I had been waiting for ten p.m.—I had an hour to go—to enter the radio contest sing for front row seats and a chance to be onstage with the hottest hip-hop and R & B sensation—Haneef!

Real talk, Haneef was putting Usher, Chris Brown, Bow Wow, and Omarion to sleep. Well . . . maybe not Chris Brown, 'cause he was kinda fly, but still—you got the point. Li'l Daddy was doin' it: six feet even, Hershey's milk chocolate skin, beautiful almond-shaped brown eyes, tight and tumbling muscles that went on into infinity, with a killah swagger like Jay-Z.

Haneef was that even-when-you-saw-it-you-still-didn't-believe-it type fine, and I was sure, every time he was on the radio, he was singing not only about me, but to me.

My best friend Naja thought I was crazy. Whatever. Cause I never said a word when she was drooling over Flavor Flav.

I looked at the clock—still a half hour to go. I decided to call Naja so we could practice what I was going to sing. As I reached for my boost mobile, it danced in my hand. It was Naja. Oh, did I mention she popped her gums before every sentence? "I've been staring at the clock," she popped, "for five hours, and it's movin' slow as hell."

"Are the batteries dying?"

"I think so, but the number on the left stays the same for like an hour. And I'm like 'Okay, you wanna move yo' ass?'" Then she popped her gums again.

I never said she wasn't an airhead, I just said she was my best friend. Naja and I had been down like four flat since kindergarten.

I didn't even comment on the clock thing. "First of all, you better fall back from my baby daddy, Haneef," I snapped. "You claimed Flavor Flav. Don't get it twisted."

"Ill, I don't want him anymore, but I do think Bobby Brown is kinda cute."

I made hurling motions with my neck. "I'ma throw up."

"You better take something, 'cause if you throw up on the phone and it flies over here . . . then we gon' have a problem."

Okay, maybe I'd missed something. "Naja, how would it fly over there?"

"Duh," she said as if I was the dumbest person on earth. "Think about it, Elite," she snapped.

"Hmmm, I just did and you know what, I don't even think I wanna know."

"The clock moved!" Naja yelled, excited. "It's ten!"

I screamed, "Okay, okay. What I'ma sing?"

"Sing," Aniyah popped her head from under the cover again, "Whatcha whatcha know bout me . . ."

I balled up my fist and said, "If you don't shut your mouth . . ."

"Puleeze," Sydney popped her eyes wide and rolled her neck. "She don't wanna sing that mess. She wanna sing, 'Let me take you to bed, lead you to places you've never been.'"

"What in the—let me find out that you been singing that mess and see what happens to you," I threatened. "Now don't let me see you pop up from the covers again."

"I'm tired of being treated like a slave," Sydney sighed.

"Be quiet!" I yelled.

"Come on," Naja snapped. "We have to hurry up. We should sing a Whitney Houston throwback. Hit all the high notes."

"Yeah, and get hung up on."

"I can sing," Naja said certain of herself. "I put Rihanna to sleep."

"Wow, that's a hard thing to do," I said sarcastically. "Look, we don't have time to argue. I'll sing, you just hum . . . softly."

We called the station at least a hundred times before we were able to get through.

"Hot 102," the DJ said. "You're on live! Who is this?"

"Ahhhhhh!!!!!!!!" Naja screamed in everybody's ear.

I swore that if we got hung up on, I was taking her drawstring weave and slinging her ass! "Would you shut up?!"

"Ladies," the DJ said, getting our attention. "This is Hot 102, and you're live on the air . . ."

"Hey," I said. "My name is Elite, and I'm from—"

"Brick City, in the house!" Naja cut me off. "I'm Naja, and I wanna give a shout out," I heard her ruffling paper in the background, "to my mother at work right now, my god brother on lockdown, and to all the homies who ain't here—"

"Naja—"

"Wait," she carried on, "and to Al-Terik, you know I'm through with you. Cause I saw you and big butt Belinda in the corner of the cafeteria—"

"Naja!"

"Dang girl, why you so rude? You know we got company on the phone."

"We're supposed to be singing!"

"Okay, and what's the problem? Sing."

"Thank you," I said, trying my best not to sound as aggravated as I felt. "Sorry about that . . . uhm . . . I wrote a song that I would like to sing—"

"Elite, they don't wanna hear no poetry."

I ignored her. "Okay, here goes. Do you want me to sing now?"

No answer.

I looked at the phone to make sure it was still on, and it was. "Hello?" My heart dropped in my chest.

No answer.

"Did they hang up?" Naja gasped.

"I think so." I couldn't believe this. "Hello?"

"Girl, they're gone. Dang, why would they do that?"

I didn't even answer. I simply hung up on her, turned on my side, and placed the covers over my head. I'm not surprised it didn't work out. Besides, my mother was a crackhead, and I knew the furthest I was probably going to get in life was from one side of my tight ass bed to the other. Tears slid down my cheeks as I closed my eyes and drifted off to sleep.

SPIN IT . . .

Track 2

"Good morning. Welcome to Hot 102," the alarm clock radio echoed throughout my room, a signal that I needed to get up and get ready for school. I turned over on my back and stared at the ceiling, where my taped poster of Haneef flapped in the top left corner and sagged in the middle.

"We're here today," the radio continued, "with hip-hop sensation Haneef."

"Wassup?! Everybody!" Haneef said and my heart palpitated.

"So," the DJ spat, filled with excitement, "today is the last day to win tickets to the Haneef concert! So, if you can sing, give me a ring!"

God must have been trying to tell me something. I reached for the house phone and dialed the radio station—they answered on the first ring.

"Hot 102. Who do we have on the line?"

"Elite!"

"Say hello to Haneef."

"I can't," I said in a pant. "I'm speechless." I heard Haneef laugh . . . and oh, he had a beautiful laugh.

"Alright," the DJ continued. "So you're calling for the contest?"

"Yes."

"Can you sing?"

"What?! Boy, don't play with me," I said seriously. "Can I sing? I sing all the time. Listen . . ." and I burst into the best soprano version of "Haaaaa . . . llelujah! Haaaaa . . . llelujah! Hallelujah, Hallelujah . . . Ha-lay-lu-yaaaaaa!"

"Oh . . . kay . . ." the DJ said. "I hope that's not what you're going to sing for us."

"Oh, no. My song is 'When You Touch Me.' It's a dedication to Haneef."

I closed my eyes, opened my mouth, and Heaven sprang from my throat. I was naturally an alto with a sultry voice like Keyshia Cole, but I had a range like Mariah Carey, so there was no mistake that I was straight killin' this contest! "I'm missing you baby . . ."

"Lee-Lee!"

Hmph. I kept singing, but I swore I heard my mother calling me by my nickname. I glanced at the clock but knew it wasn't her, because at that time of the morning she was sleeping off her high from the night before.

"Miss when you touch me . . ." I continued to sing.

"Lee-Lee!"

My eyes popped wide open. That was my mother.

"Elite Juliana Parker, get yo' fresh ass off this phone, talkin' crazy?!"

"Ma, get off the phone! I'm doing this to win tickets for Haneef!"

"Haneef?! Who the hell is Haneef, some li'l hoodlum ass drug dealer? All you can do for Haneef right now is get his chin checked. You up here singing like you hot in the ass about somebody touching you! Keep on singing, and it's gon' be me reaching out to touch that ass! If anything, you need to ask Haneef if he got two dollars I can borrow. If not, then get yo' ass off my line!"

Something told me . . . I had just died. I hung up the phone, laid back on my bed, and watched my Haneef poster fall straight on my head.

A half hour into gettin' my misery on, I rose from the floor, showered, and dressed in a pair of fitted Juicy jeans, a V-neck tee, colorful bangles, and matching earrings.

When I walked in the living room, I saw that either my mother had found two dollars to borrow or she'd stolen something to supplement it, because she wasn't around anymore. Cassie Parker was one hot blazed-up mess.

She raised us from behind the bathroom door most of our lives because that was where she hid to get high, as if we really didn't know what was going on. And when she got with her new zooted-up boyfriend, Gary, they took crack love to the streets. Most of the time she was either in somebody's hallway, a street corner, or an abandoned building.

I'd never had the type of home where my friends came over and kicked it in my room. As a matter of fact, the only ones who knew the real life I lived were Naja and Jahaad (my boyfriend). Everybody else knew nothing. And I wanted to keep it that way. The last thing I needed was a buncha chicks or the state in my business. I had adjusted to being the "real" mother around this place, and it was cool.

I loved my sisters and brothers, and whatever it took to keep my family together was what I was going to do.

And about my father: the shit was so typical. He just wasn't around.

Needless to say, I was nothing special. So . . . it was what it was, and other than having been played (twice) like too sweet Kool-Aid for Haneef tickets, I didn't complain. What was the use? I'd never known shit to change because I complained. Which was why I kept it movin' around my house.

I walked over to the pull-out couch, where my brother Ny'eem was asleep, and said, "Get yo' ass up!"

He sucked his teeth and ruffled the sheets, but did I look fazed? Puleeze!

"And don't think," I carried on, "that I don't

know what time you came in here last night. Play with me if you want to, and you'll be down at the men's shelter or juvie somewhere."

"Shut up!" he snapped and stretched. "You always tryna be somebody's mother."

"I'm the best mother you got."

"What?" He stood from the couch and looked down in my face. He was only fifteen, but he towered over me by at least three inches. "Girl, I'm grown."

Grown? Was this suckah tryna buck? Okay, I saw where this is going. I stood up on a rusted metal chair that had somehow ended up as part of our décor and struck a karate pose, lifting my leg high enough so that if I had wanted to, I could have taken it to his chest.

And he cracked up laughing. He laughed so hard that tears fell from his eyes. "You think I'm funny? Do I look like I'm laughing to you?"

"No, you look like you lost your mind." And he left me standing there.

"You just get ready for school!" I yelled behind him. "And let me even hear a whisper that you've been skipping class again and see what I really do to you."

Just as I stepped down from the chair, my five-year-old brother, Mica, rushed out of the bathroom with a sheet wrapped around his neck, like he and Superman were boys. "What the hell? Boy, where are your school clothes?"

"I'm not wearing that shit!"

"Hol' up . . . hol' up . . . don't you cuss again!" I balled up my fist. Mica was the one I really had to bring it to, 'cause he thought he was tough, but if I looked at him hard and long enough, he'd burst into tears. "Go put on those clothes. As much money as I paid that booster! I work at the mall part-time—"

"Mommy gets a welfare check."

"And Mommy gettin' high, too," Ny'eem snapped as he gathered his clothes for the day.

"Shut up!" I said to Ny'eem. "Now," I turned my attention back to Mica, "why don't you want to wear what I laid out for you?"

"Because I want my pants to droop down like Ny'eem's. You got a belt laid out for me, some hard-bottom shoes, and a turtleneck. I may as well be going to church."

"I didn't lay out a turtleneck for you. It's a Phat Farm shirt. Know what, I don't have to argue with you." I stared him down and just like I predicted, he was in tears.

"Everybody treats me like a baby around here!" And he stormed back into the bathroom.

Whatever. I didn't have time to listen to that, so I returned to my room, where the twins had to be watched closely when they put on their gear. Otherwise, they'd be happy to walk out of the house draped in my bebe, Baby Phat, or any other designer dig I had either worked or gotten a hook up for.

And yes, they looked a hot mess, considering I was five foot five and a size ten, and they were just eight years old. So, I stood guard while they slipped on their jeans, cute li'l Bobby Jack shirts, and some pink and white kicks.

Their hair was shoulder-length and easy to maintain because for ten dollars, every other week the girl across the hall put it in cornrows and beads. An hour after me acting like Jerome the flashlight cop, everybody was ready to roll.

We took one bus but got off at different stops for our respective schools. The twins, Mica, and Nyeem got off at the first stop and mine was last.

As soon as the city bus doors opened and I stepped foot in front of the school, I knew right away that everyone had heard me get played on the radio. Especially since they all looked at me and either smiled too wide or laughed in my face.

But it was all good, 'cause I was too ready to read these ghetto birds like they stole somethin'. Besides, just because I had a jacked-up home life, didn't mean I wasn't fly—because I was. Honey colored skin, flat-ironed straight hair that draped past my shoulders, Asian eyes, full lips, thick hips, and a cover girl smile.

Just when my boost mobile vibrated through my purse, I saw Naja run toward me. I twisted my MAC-covered lips and ignored her. Yes, I was still pissed.

I flipped my phone open. "Who dis?"

"Elite?" It was a male voice.

"Yeah."

"Wassup, girl?"

"Terrance? Boy, didn't I tell you to lose yourself?!" Terrance was a boy who pushed up on me once at the bus stop. I called myself tryin' to creep, but every time I turned around he was on my line. Can you say stalker?

"This isn't Terrance. This is DJ Twan from Hot 102."

"Yeah, right."

"Didn't you call us this morning for the singing contest?"

"Oh, now you got jokes, Terrance? Look, I'm down to my last twenty minutes on my phone, so I don't have time to waste with you on my line. Now bounce!"

"Elite, this is Haneef. Your friend, Naja, called the station when we announced that despite your mother playing us both out, you won the contest. Front row seats to the concert and a chance to be onstage with me!"

I tapped my foot and looked around at the sea of students going into the school. Then I looked at Naja, who was standing here grinnin', mushed her dead in the head, and poked my finger in the center of the bubble she was prepared to pop.

"Do I sound impressed? I know you don't think I'm going to believe that this is Haneef, and you all cared about me so much that you gon' track me down, for what? Puleeze, this is Terrance. And since you playing so many games, I'ma be sure to tell all your boys on the basketball team that you ain't never had no booty, punk ass!"

"This is the last time," a deep male voice said, "before we hang up—"

"Do you—if this is really Haneef, then sing something."

Suddenly the phone turned into a personal serenade: "If I don't have you baby, I'ma go crazy . . . need you in my life."

It was at that moment I knew it was Haneef. "Jesus!" I screamed, right before I looked at Naja, who was jumping up and down.

"This *is* Haneef!" I screamed at the top of my lungs.

"Yes," he said. "You won the contest, and your friend Naja is the one to thank! So, do you want the tickets? There're two of them, so you can bring her with you!"

"Boy," I said seriously. "Don't play with me."

"Come to the station by tomorrow and pick them up," the DJ said.

Naja and I hugged tightly as we jumped up and down.

"Haneef!" Naja yelled, smushing her cheek against mine and trying to speak into the phone. "My cousin's baby mother, god sister, aunt's brother, and li'l sister, Tasia said they know you, and to tell you wassup! I love you, Haneef!"

I shot Naja the eye and mouthed, "You're going to make them hang up again!"

"Elite!" the DJ seemed to be ignoring Naja. "Tell us the best station in Jersey!"

"Hot 102! Where my baby daddy lives! Holl-laaaah!"

Once we were off the line, Naja and I started screaming again. "Okay, okay," I said. "We need to calm down."

We took a deep breath, looked around, and every li'l pigeon out there was staring in our direction. It was obvious they were sweatin' us. Naja and I started smiling in their direction while giving them our famous Miss America waves. I saw just by the green oozing from their hater type glare that they were dying to be fly with us. After the phone call I just had, we were officially groupie royalty.

After a few minutes of pleasing our court, we sauntered into Arts High, side by side, both of us throwing our right shoulders forward and strutting down the hall. There was no mistaking that we had arrived . . .

"Oh, you just gon' play me on the radio," halted me in my spot. I closed my eyes and I knew by the voice it was Jahaad. I was so high off Haneef that I'd almost forgotten this dude existed.

"Get over here!" he said as he turned me around and pulled me toward him. It was written all over his face that he was pissed. He was mean, muggin' the heck outta me, and the look alone almost made me promise to behave.

Jahaad was the spitting image of Usher: the

color of pecan, chestnut brown eyes, five eleven, and athletically built.

He was looking at me with disdain—he was still cute—but obviously pissed. He was dressed like a rock star with slightly baggy jeans, a thin silver link chain hanging from his belt to his back pocket, a black short sleeve Korn tee, and an off-white thermal underneath.

We'd been together since ninth grade but since we'd been in the eleventh grade, I had gotten tired of him. But he had been my first, and I didn't exactly know what life would have been like without him. He nagged the heck outta me, always accused me of cheating, complained all the time, always had something smart to say, and argued all day if he could have . . . but other than that . . . he'd always had a way of being there when I needed him.

I snatched away from him. "What I tell you about pulling on me?!"

"We need to handle this, Elite?" Naja asked, looking Jahaad up and down.

"No, Naja, we're straight," I assured her.

"Ai'ight." She pointed down the hall, where a group of our girls were. "Hollah if you need me." Naja walked backwards down the hall, eyeing Jahaad the entire way.

"What I tell you about grabbing me?!" I snapped.

"And what I tell you about not listening?! I see I've been too nice to you."

Too nice. I gave him the screw face, and it was obvious by that comment that he'd been listening to some chick. "Ciera been in your face again?" I said more as an accusation than a question.

"Don't worry about Ciera!" he snapped. "Worry about you. All on the radio, being a groupie ass ho!"

"What? Who you callin' a ho?" I screeched. I may have been a groupie, but I wasn't no ho. "You a ho, as a matter of fact. You come from a long line of skeezers!"

"You talkin' about my mama?"

"Well, I wasn't gon' call no name, but if the spandex fits!"

"Are you crazy, talking to me like this?"

"Boy, if you don't get yo' wannabe Billy bad ass outta my way . . . !"

"Are you crazy, playing me for some punk ass cat who wouldn't even know you if you sat next to him? He must've heard you were easy and that's the real reason why he tracked you down."

Easy? He called me easy? "If I was easy, I'd be givin' you some booty, Mr. I-don't-wear-condoms. Easy? Last I checked, you were ridin' the pole."

"And you wonder why other chicks be checkin' me—because you don't know how to treat me."

"So, what you sayin'? You tryna get with one of them? What, Ciera tryna ride yo' impacted ass sack. I wish you would leave me and try and get with that dog ass chick!"

I was so pissed, I could've smacked him upside

his head. There had been rumors about this pigeon, Ciera, trying to kick it with Jahaad on the low. And word was that she was checkin' for him mad hard, and that occasionally—on the D.L.—this fool was trickin' all his li'l Burger King money on her bama ass.

Needless to say, I had to secure my place, regardless of how I really felt about staying in a relationship with this dude. But the mere thought of this chick being in my man's face drove me crazy.

So, I had to let her know to stay outta my way before I laid her ass out cold. Point blank, period. It didn't matter that I didn't want him anymore. What mattered was that as long as I knew she wanted him, I wasn't gon' leave him.

And this wasn't because I was selfish; I was so not above sharing the wealth. And usually I wasn't a hater, and uhmmm . . . maybe, if someone other than my archenemy had come along, then I would've put Jahaad on the block. But with Ciera on the loose, it wasn't gon' happen.

"Now, I don't know about anybody else, but Jahaad's girl," Jahaad spat while pointing his finger in my face, "don't be acting like this! Now, unless you want some other chick to take your spot, you'll get your act together. Feel me?"

"I really don't appreciate the way you're talking to me!" I pointed my finger back in his face.

"Well, you should get your act together."

"So what you sayin'? I ain't your girl no more?"

"You my girl, but if you keep acting like this . . ."

"Acting like this, and what? As long as we've been together, you don't think any more of me than to be spittin' whatever your boys or some bum bitch done told you to say to me?! Yeah, maybe you're right. Maybe I don't need to be your girl." I turned to storm away but he snatched me back around.

"Don't be like that, Elite. I'm sorry." He stroked my cheek. "I know I'm buggin', but when I think about losing you, I just don't know what to do. It's like you think it's alright to play me or something."

"You know it wasn't even like that," I said, thinking now was really as good a time as ever to dump him. "I was just . . . just excited."

"Yeah, over another dude. And you know he doesn't love you like me. Nobody will ever love you like I do."

"I know," I said in my best sorrow-filled voice.

"So then you ain't going to the concert, right?"

"What?" I quickly snapped. "Boy, don't play with me."

Jahaad looked at me as if he could see right through me. "You better not go to that concert! You better not try me."

"Excuse you?"

"So you gon' just disrespect me?"

"I'm not disrespecting you! I'm just going to a concert!"

"So what you sayin', to hell with me?!"

I sighed.

"Oh," he snapped. He was so mad I swore I saw smoke coming from his nose. "Seems your mind is made up. Ai'ight, deuce-deuce. I'm out, and don't call me, either!" He pounded two fingers on his chest and walked away. Something he'd never done, despite how many arguments we'd had.

I felt like a mannequin. I swear I couldn't move from my spot. I couldn't believe he'd actually left me standing here and had walked off, disappearing like thin vapor into a sea of students.

Suddenly the bell rang and people started rushing past me, saying, "Elite! I heard you on the radio. I can't believe you really won those tickets!"

A few more said, "Wish I could go."

"Well, ya can't!" Naja slipped over to me, grabbed me by the arm, and practically dragged me down the hall to class.

SPIN IT . . .

Track 3

Okay, so Jahaad had left me in the middle of the hallway, and unless I planned on not going to the concert, my relationship was going to be over. This might have been the easy way out . . . letting him dump me and not the other way around.

And maybe a week before, I would've seized the moment, but then again maybe I wouldn't have, especially since this was the first time I faced the real possibility that he might actually leave me. So I had no choice but to figure out how I was going to keep Jahaad and go to the concert at the same time.

Not able to come up with a clear and concise plan, I shook my head. I was at work, just starting my shift. I checked my work schedule and saw that I had the night of the concert off. Not that I thought that would be a problem, considering my manager, Thelma, was cool. Last year she made me assistant manager and once I saw the jump in my paycheck, I told her I would forever be grateful and do whatever she wanted me to. Which I did. I always closed up, and every other weekend I opened, did extra hours, and always made the schedule so she wouldn't have to.

I had been working at bebe in the Mall at Short Hills every other day after school and on the weekends since I forged my mother's signature (at fourteen) on my working papers. I was tired of rockin' the crackhead kid's look: dingy and too big clothes, no frill kicks, and a smirk on my face that screamed this was the best I could do. Hell, there was no need for the truth to be that obvious when I could work and lie about it.

Anywho, I already explained to Ny'eem that if he wanted me to get those Air Force Ones he'd been eyeing, then he had to be home on time tomorrow night to keep the kids. Otherwise, his dreams of being sneaker king would be a wrap. Especially since I'm going back on my word of not getting him anything, since he refuses to get a J.O.B.

I had to admit I was worried I was gonna lose Ny'eem to the streets. All he wanted to do was hang out on the corner with his boys and chase behind them. Everybody, except Ny'eem of course, saw they were up to no good.

My mother even told him that if she caught him hanging on the corner again, she was going to wreck shop on the block. And if she did, that would have been on him. And I tried to tell him not to sleep on Cassie—between her lovemaking sessions with the pipe, she did try to be somebody's mama. Not mine though, because ever since I had to mother my sisters and brothers, I told her to be clear: I was grown.

"Okay, Naja." I looked toward Naja, who's worked with me since last summer. "We're not on the schedule tomorrow, but we have extra hours next week to make up for it." We walked over to the counter and I stood behind the cash register while she leaned up against the front of the counter.

"That's if I'm not married," Naja said with ease.

This chick was crazy, and the way I was looking at her told her that I thought so. "What are you talking about?!" I couldn't help but laugh.

"Girl, please. I heard Rick Ross is going to be there, and if so, I'm stripping on site." She started throwing her arms in the air and dropping down low. "'Drop down and sweep the floor wit' it'—hey'yayyy!" She popped back up. "I am nothing," she popped her gums and snapped her fingers in a Z-motion, "to play with."

"You so crazy," I giggled. "But look, what we gon' wear?"

"Girl, I got this fly Juicy Couture outfit. And let me tell you it makes my boobs look like hey'yay, my ass look like holl'laaaah! And my stilettos look like they sing, 'Here comes Miss America . . .'" Naja strutted like Naomi Campbell from one side of the boutique to the other as if she were working a Paris runway, did a pose, and came back again. "I'm puttin' er'body to sleep. Except my girl, of course. We can be on the same level of flyness. What you buy?"

I sighed. I hated admitting this . . . even to Naja. "I don't have any extra money this week. I had to pay for the twins' school pictures, Mica's school trip, and I had to buy Ny'eem a bus card. I'm broke. And all I have left is like fifty dollars."

"Dang, that ain't hardly enough and you need five dollars added to that just to get your nails and feet done. We can make arrangements with Tamara down the hall from you to do your hair. What about the booster, Lisa?"

"She got locked up last week."

"Damn, and you know you definitely can't wear no old gear."

"Maybe though," I said hopeful, "no one we know will be there."

"Elite, this is the biggest concert of the year. Everybody and their stepmama will be there."

"I know . . . maybe . . . you know . . . I shouldn't—"

"Girl, I know you ain't about to trip like maybe you shouldn't go?" She sighed. "Damn, Elite, so what we gon' do?" She placed both elbows on the counter and put her chin in her palms. "I got it," she popped her head up and said as if a lightbulb had just gone off. "Maybe . . . you know, hmph."

"Would you just tell me!"

She popped her gums, "Why don't—nah, you won't do it."

"What?" I said, aggravated.

"Nah, you won't do it."

"What?!"

"Nah."

"Would you say it! I hate when people do that!"

"Okay, since you beggin' and everything." She laughed. "Why don't you know, you borrow a li'l sumthin'-sumthin' from the store?"

"What store? This store?"

"Uhmm hmm."

I waved my hand—it was obvious she'd lost her mind. "You crazy as hell. And who gon' come bail me out when I go to jail? My mother is a crack-head—she done smoked all the bail money away. Girl please, you buggin'."

"Look, you're the assistant manager. You can delete the tape, take the gear, and bring it back after the concert if you'd like. It's nothin'. That's why I said borrow, and if it'll make you feel better, I'll borrow something, too."

"I'm not—" I was interrupted by my cell phone ringing. It was Jahaad and I sent his ass straight to voicemail. I didn't feel like being aggravated with an argument. And besides, he knew my minutes were low. "Now, Naja, back to you—"

"Oh look," a female voice interrupted me. "I do believe we know the hired help." When we looked toward the door, it was Ciera.

"Is this the part where I punch her in the face," Naja said, more as a statement than a question.

Ciera rolled her eyes. "Anyway," she said to her crew, "I have backstage passes." She wiggled her neck as she looked through the racks. "And my cousin on my father's side, his god sister's brother manages Haneef, so you know we gon' get V.I.P. treatment."

"And you talkin' 'bout wearin' some old shit," Naja mumbled. "Please, I wish you would."

Ciera carried on, "And I didn't have to call the radio station beggin' for tickets." She peeped over at me and waved. "Hey Elite, hey Naja. I thought I recognized you two. Wassup with y'all?"

"Nothing," Naja said, and I ignored her.

"Hey, Elite, can't speak?" she asked as her Supremes stood behind her and twisted their necks to confirm she'd asked me a question, shooting me looks like I'd better answer.

"Exactly," I snapped. "I can't speak."

"Whatever," she flicked her hand as her phone rang. "Typical behavior of a hater . . . hello?" she answered while staring at me. "Hey, Jahaad . . ."

Jahaad? This bitch was trippin'.

"Jahaad?" Naja looked at me. "Is that your Jahaad?"

I tried to play it off because truthfully I didn't know. "Girl, please. Does Ciera look as if she want it wit' me. Heck no, that's not my Jahaad. Besides, he's too stuck on me to even go the skeezer route."

"Don't sleep on hos and tricks," Naja warned.

"Whatever. Anyway, as I was saying, I'm not stealing," I whispered.

"It's borrowing, and what if you make it onstage with Haneef? You doggon' well got to be beyond fly, and not some average everyday mall fly, but bebe-va-va-voom fly. Especially if you wanna get selected to sing."

"Naja . . . I just don't know."

"Hold it. I know you not gon' let this rainbow shop skeezer play you? Come on, Elite, you gotta come better than that."

She had a point.

"And look at that heifer—" she carried on.

"I'ma get this," Ciera said. "And I'ma rock this with my Fendi heels and bag—"

"And on top of that you gon' let that ho steal yo' man?" Naja continued. "She's already put the moves on Jahaad, so you know you beat for Haneef if she gets next to him."

She had a point again. "So if I borrow it, you think Thelma will notice?" I asked reluctantly.

"No, just bring it back the next day and act as if someone returned them."

"True."

"All I'm saying is don't get played to the left by some ghetto bird." She nodded toward Ciera, who was eyeing the very outfit I had wanted all week.

"Ooule, I like this." Ciera held up the hip hugging jeans and champagne halter with the braided strap. "Oh, this is fly."

“Now what you gon’ do?” Naja twisted her lips.

“I’ma borrow it,” I said, still unsure.

“Ai’ight, cool, so let me go collect your gear.” Naja walked over to Ciera. “Oh, my God, girl. This stuff is irregular, you don’t need this. If you wear this, it’s gon’ turn you into even more of a hot barnyard ass mess. Let me take this from you.” She snatched it out of Ciera’s hand and then proceeded to remove the rest of the clothes from the rack and take them in the back.

Ciera stood there stunned. “What in the—know what, I don’t have to take this. I can go someplace else.” And she stormed out of the store.

“Bye!” I waved. “See you at the concert!”

SPIN IT . . .

Track 4

I was always welcome at the Throwbacks, a.k.a the Joneses. Naja's house. Where the only place time changed was on the outside. True story—Naja's family were the nicest people on the block, but I always thought somebody, somewhere along the lines, jacked them up. All her dad, who everybody called Nephew (why? I don't know), said was "Yup-Yup," "Word up," and "You gots to chill." And her mother, Neecy—could you say leg warmers, spandex, tube tops, and two-tone jeans? She was the black version of Cyndi Lauper, the ancient eighties in the flesh.

And her grandmother, Mom-Mom, made everybody call her Delicious, was senile, and told everybody she was a retired stripper. Oh, and she thought everybody on TV was real.

"Ma!" Naja screamed. "Come and get Mom-Mom. She's screaming at another repeat!"

"They keep doing the same things to me!" Mom-Mom screamed. "Over and over again! I swear to Gawd, I'm 'bout to straight Crip on a fool!" She threw her fingers in the air and started crossing them. For a moment it looked as if her hands were having a seizure. "East side!"

Neecy pushed Naja's room door open, "Come on, Mom-Mom."

"My name is Delicious, and I'm a retired stripper."

"Come on, Delicious," Neecy said, shaking her head.

Immediately, Mom-Mom dropped down and started getting her eagle on. "Where is a pole when you need one?"

"You're embarrassing Naja," Neecy said as she grabbed Mom-Mom's hand and ushered her out of the room.

"Naja," I whispered as Neecy closed the door behind them. "Has your grandmother always been like that?"

"Like what?"

"You know, senile."

"Oh, she's not senile, she's from North Carolina. She crazy as hell, but she's not senile."

Why did I bother? "Can I use your phone?"

"Yeah," Naja said as she proceeded to get dressed. I dialed my house and Sydney answered.

Mica was screaming in the background. "Syd, what is wrong with him?"

"Aniyah did it. He asked her was there was really a Santa Claus and she told him no, Santa got capped last year. And the next thing I know, he's all tangled up in that Superman sheet he wears, having a nervous breakdown."

"Let me speak to him."

"Mica!" she yelled. "Elite on the phone."

"Si-si-sistah," he sniffled as he spoke into the phone. "Santa—Santa—Santa . . ."

"Mica, it's October. Why are you worried about Santa?"

"Oh God—oh God—he got shot."

"He did not!" I said sternly. "Now you stop crying and get yourself together. You're a big boy."

"Yeah, Mica," Aniyah said in the background. "Santa didn't get shot. He's in a halfway house."

"Aniyah! Put Aniyah on this phone!"

"Yeah?" she said, getting on the line.

"You better stop! Now look, Ny'eem should be home any minute. I'ma be home late."

"Okay. Should we put the extra lock on the door to keep Mommy and Gary out until you come back?"

I looked at the calendar before I answered the question. First of the month. "Mommy won't be home for a minute, so you'll be alright. Just remember what I said, and stop teasing Mica."

"All right," she snickered. "I will."

Once I hung up, I proceeded to get dressed in

my fitted bebe jeans, champagne colored halter, open toe stilettos, and instead of flat-ironing my hair, I let it drape over my shoulders in an abundance of ocean waves. I was too fly for words. And I decided to heck with the disguise. Jahaad will just have to live with me going to the concert and gettin' my groove on!

Naja placed her hands on her hips. She rocked a pair of fitted Juicy jeans with a matching rhinestone hoodie, and heels. We pranced out of her room and stopped in the living room.

"Daddy," she said, "How do we look?"

"Yup-Yup."

"That means," her mother chimed in, "that you real fly."

"And you know this," Naja smiled. "Okay Ma, we're going to the concert."

"You need a ride?" We both looked at her mother in her too small purple spandex leggings, white tube top, and platforms. "Nah, we're good," Naja and I said at practically the same time.

"Okay, but if you need a ride, hollah."

"Bye, Ma!"

"Bye, y'all."

"Bye, Daddy!"

"You gots to chill," he smiled.

"Bye, Mom-Mom—"

Mom-Mom screamed, "It's Delicious!"

SPIN IT . . .

Track 5

"Oh . . . hell . . . to da nawl!" Naja yelled as we sat in the front row at Continental Arena, feeling like hip-hop princesses and looking twice as fly. "Is that," she continued, "Lil Wayne hugged up on Trina?" Naja shoved her soda in my hand, causing the ice in the cup to rattle about. "Here, hold this, 'cause in a minute it's about to be on and poppin'. How Lil Wayne gon' take her back?"

Naja stood up from her seat and I snatched her back down. "What the—?" She was outta pocket! "Gurl, you straight trippin'. you can't go runnin' up on Lil Wayne!"

"Why not? He can get it, too. I don't believe this." For a minute I thought she had tears in her eyes. "I can't believe Lil Wayne didn't wait for me."

"Wait for you?" *Was this fool crazy?*

"Yeah."

Was she sniffling? Hold it . . . I knew that couldn't be a tear I saw.

"After," she sniffed, "I didn't make the second season of *Flavor of Love,* I wrote Lil Wayne and told him we were meant to be and that I'd be eighteen next year, so he should wait for me . . . And here he is, gettin' it in wit' Trina? Knowing she was droppin' it for Young Buck, too? I swear, nobody listens to Kya or 50 Cent."

All I did was stare. There were no words for her. It was official: Naja's common sense was twisted.

"This is some bullshit, you know that, right?" Naja wiped her eyes, then looked to the side of us and stared as if she'd just seen a ghost. "Wait . . . a minute . . . wait . . . a minute. Didn't I tell that big head ho to stay away from my man?!" Naja whipped her neck toward me. "Oh it's 'bout to be a misunderstanding."

"You need to calm down before you blow something."

"Oh, I'ma blow something alright." She pounded her fist at Rihanna.

"Keep it up and they gon' arrest you."

I wasn't sure what she said in response because the lights went down and the crowd started screaming. Lloyd, Haneef's opening act, took the stage and Naja started panting, "Lloyd! I love you! It's me, it's Naja, I call your record company every day! I'm all over your MySpace page. Did you get my friend request?! I wanna be your number one friend. Lloyd, did you get my email?!"

"Would you shut up?!" I'd thought I was the world's best groupie, but all along, my best friend had me beat.

Lloyd and the crowd were singing his hit song together. People were yelling and screaming, and some girls were even crying. His band was fantastic and just as he went to sing his last song, Jordin Sparks joined him on stage.

"Oh hell, no, he didn't?!" Naja snapped. "I know he didn't bypass me for *American Idol*'s rendition of Big Bird?"

"Now you need to apologize for that," I said surprised. "You know she can sing!"

"Well, if singing is what matters, then why is Rihanna with Chris Brown?"

I ignored her. I'd had enough of her insulting people. Once she saw I was ignoring her, she started enjoying the concert and singing along. As Lloyd and his entourage left the stage, Trey Songz hopped on and Naja passed out.

I fanned her. "You better learn to breathe again, because here comes Haneef!" She sat up and we both started screaming. The entire place went completely black, and then spotlights shot back and forth across the audience.

Everyone was yelling and holding up their lighters and flashlights, the streams of light and flickering flames seemed to illuminate the sky. Girls were crying, "I love you, Haneef!"

"Hmph," I shouted. "Not like I do!"

Naja and I started bumping shoulders and throwing our arms in the air as the dancers came on-stage and did some of the flyest hip-hop moves I'd ever seen. And right when they were in the midst of gettin' down wit' the get down, a spotlight streamed center stage, and there was a cloud of smoke and an array of helicopter noises.

"Attention," a computerized male voice radiated the arena. "Calling all cars—calling all cars—hip-hop sensation Haneef—is wanted . . ." The voice repeated itself, Haneef was lowered onto the stage, and the crowd went ballistic!

Naja and I were screaming at the top of our lungs as Haneef started dancing and singing my favorite song, "All for You."

"Jeeeeee'susssssss!!!!!!" I started to hyperventilate. I looked to see where fresh air could be found, and guess who was staring right in my face? You guessed it: Ciera.

I rolled my eyes, like chick, please, and commenced to getting my groove on again.

I couldn't believe this was happening to me and for the first time in my life, I forgot about all the adult responsibilities I had. And instead of feeling grown, I knew then, like at no other time in my life, that that was what seventeen was supposed to feel like.

Haneef sang three songs: one remix, one from his new album, and a throwback. Afterwards, he slowed the music down and started talking to the audience, while his band continued to play in the background. "Jersey! How's everybody tonight?!"

The crowd shouted, "Alright!" in response.

"Y'all look good out there!" He shielded his hands over his eyes like a visor and looked into the audience. "Well, on the radio yesterday I promised I would bring a hottie onstage with me to sing. Y'all ready for that?"

"Yeah!" the crowd shouted back.

I started cheesin'and Najah whispered, "Look at Ciera."

Ciera was straightening her clothes and hair as if she were sure her name was going to be called.

"And I decided," Haneef said, "to let my homeboy Chris Brown pull out a name for me."

Chris Brown walked onstage and Naja screamed, "I love you, Chris! To hell with Rihanna! It's all about me and you! I love you!"

Chris Brown reached into a spinning barrel of names and handed one to Haneef.

Ciera stood up and mouthed to her friends, "Told you," then proceeded to wink at me.

"Elite Parker!" Haneef said into the microphone, while shielding his eyes again. "Come on and rock this with me!"

"What did he say?" Had he just called my name?

"Elite," he repeated.

I looked around. Had he really just called my name?

"Is Elite here tonight?" he asked again.

"Right here!" Naja pointed, pushing me on the shoulder. "Right here, this is my best friend! She is just like my sister! Here she is, right here!"

Security came over, placed a microphone headset on me, and that's when I knew the moment was for real. I screamed in excitement at the top of my lungs.

Once onstage, Haneef walked over and grabbed my hand, then started slow dancing with me, and the next thing I knew he was singing, "Rather fall in love with a girl that's made for me . . ." and on he went.

I was in such a daze that I forgot about the duet, until he nodded at me. "Oh," I pointed to myself, "I guess it's my turn." My hands were shaking like crazy and usually I was never nervous when it came to singing. Heck, I can't count the number of drug dealers I sang for to get my mama some free crack.

I took a deep breath and let my voice flow. "And who knew you would find a girl like me . . ." I thought my voice had cracked or something because the crowd went silent, and even Haneef looked shocked.

It was official. I was dead and my dreams of being a star had been buried along with me. But just when I thought all hope was lost, the crowd suddenly lost control and started edging me on. All I could hear was: "Sing! Get it, girl. You workin' it!"

I continued to sing and Haneef kept staring at me. It felt sort of strange because something in his eyes said his stare meant more than just tryin' to please a fan.

* * *

Haneef had gotten at least three cues that I had been onstage too long, but he ignored them. By the time we were done, everyone was on their feet giving us a standing ovation, and Naja was on the sidelines shouting, "That's my girl!"

I couldn't believe this was happening to me. For once, my life was perfect.

"Make sure you come see me backstage." Haneef kissed me on the forehead as security escorted me back to my seat.

For the next hour and a half the concert remained off da hook, and all I could do was bask in the kiss that Haneef placed on my forehead. I didn't know about Naja, but I was thinking they might have to physically remove me from that place, because the way I felt, I might never leave.

Immediately after the concert ended, everyone who had backstage passes lined up. Naja and I rushed over. I was on cloud nine and Naja was bragging about how well she and I sang. I looked at her. "Last I checked, I was the one singing."

"Oh, you ain't hear me?" she asked surprised. "Listen, I was singing like this, 'Ahhhhhhhhhh . . .'"

Oh, God, her voice was cracking. "It's cool, yeah, I heard you."

"No, seriously," she insisted. "I've gotten better."

"Uhmm hmmm, I know," I said as I felt my cell phone vibrating in my pocket. "Dang, who is this?"

As I pulled out my phone, security started rushing us to the front. I saw Haneef talking to a fan and taking pictures. I was so amped, I forgot the phone was ringing. I looked at the caller ID and saw it was someone calling me from home. Oh heck, no. I wanted to say voicemail.

We slowly moved closer to Haneef and dang, this phone was vibrating again. I pulled it out and flipped it open.

"Elite!" Sydney screamed. "Everybody in here is dead!"

"What?!" My heart jumped in my chest.

"Er'body. Aniyah, Mica, and me. Can't you hear it in my voice? Don't I sound dead?"

"You're not dead!"

"We are dead. We haven't eaten all day since the bologna they served us at school and it's going on midnight."

I looked at security and they told me to put away the phone. "Where is Ny'eem?" I asked.

"Ny'eem hasn't been here at all and we're starving. Here, listen to Mica."

I heard Mica in the background moaning, "I'm dead. Somebody help me. I'm dead."

"Please, Elite," she begged softly. "Mommy and Gary are here held up in the bathroom, and Mommy just sold the last carton of eggs we had to the girl down the hall. So we need you. You know Mommy and Gary listen to you, and I gotta go to the bathroom."

I couldn't believe this. I was this close to meeting Haneef and had to turn around. I swallowed. "Alright, I'm on my way."

I looked at Naja. "Girl, you go on, but I need to go and get with my sisters and brothers."

"Oh, okay, do you." She waved and didn't even look my way. I held my head down and walked out of the arena.

A few seconds later I heard, "Elite! Elite!" I turned around and it was Naja.

"I was just playing, girl. You know I'm not gon' do you like that."

And as we waited for the bus, we carried on about how much fun we'd just had.

I spent my last five dollars on buying a box of chicken from Crown Royal on Elizabeth Avenue and then split it with the twins and Mica. Ny'eem still hadn't come home and honestly, I didn't even care. I mean, I cared, but I was tired of caring and him taking advantage of it.

After feeding Mica and the twins, I made them go to bed and attempted to stay up and wait for Ny'eem. Of course it was to no avail, because the next thing I heard was my mother's voice, seducing me out of my sleep.

"Elite. Elite, wake up." I opened one eye and looked at the clock: two a.m. "Wake up." My mother was now shaking my thigh.

"I don't have two dollars." I closed my eyes and threw my legs over the side of the sofa. I felt like

I'd just slammed my ankles into a brick wall, but when I looked to see, it was a sleeping Ny'eem. I'd hit him on the shoulder, but he didn't wake up, and all he did was stir. I swear I felt like kicking him.

"I don't want two dollars," my mother snapped. "I wanna know how the concert was."

I turned back to face her. "How'd you know about the concert?"

"Ny'eem told me. Right before I chased his ass off the corner. He said you sang onstage. Said that some of his friends was there and that you ripped it!"

"Ma!" I said, recapturing the excitement. "I was in heaven. And I was singing so tough that it silenced the crowd."

"What?!" she jumped up. "Get the hell outta here!"

"Yeah, and I think Haneef couldn't even believe it."

"Haneef?" she sat back down on the floor. "Is that—"

"Ma, he not some street hustler. He's a pop star."

"Okay, 'cause you know I don't want no nonsense."

For a moment I stared at her and wondered what it would be like to have her like this all the time, and not have to share her with the crack pipe, Gary, or the streets. I knew she loved me and that she cared, but something inside her stopped her from caring enough to be sober. And it was only in these few stolen moments that I even remembered she had real motherly instinct. "I know you don't want any nonsense, Ma."

"I hope you do, because you're special, Elite. That's why I named you Elite. Because you're the best, and I don't want nobody messing up your future. I don't want none of y'all to be like me."

After an awkward moment of silence and me thinking of how I had very little memories of my mother being sober, she cleared her throat and said, "So tell me what happened, from beginning to end." She was sounding more like a seventeen-year-old friend than my mother.

I lay back with my head on the armrest, stared at the ceiling, and recapped for her the magical night that I'd had.

Afterwards we laughed, joked, and even sang. She had the prettiest voice I'd ever heard. On a good day, she would have put Whitney Houston to sleep.

I hadn't had a night like this in a long time. It almost made not being able to meet Haneef backstage and Aniyah calling me up to announce that everybody in the house was dead worth it.

I didn't remember falling asleep, all I knew was that when I opened my eyes, the sun was shining into the living room and the spot where my mother was sitting was empty. For a moment I wondered if the conversation we'd had the night before was even real.

SPIN IT . . .

Track 6

It was official: I was the bomb and er'body in Arts High was checkin' for me, especially since I rocked the Haneef concert the night before.

"Elite!" my portentous fans screamed. "I heard you killed it!" Everywhere I went, that's all I heard: homeroom, honors english, trigonometry, economics, music, and on it went. "Elite this and Elite that!" My li'l taste of Hollywood—or should I say—hollyhood—had me zooted.

Which is why when the school day ended and Naja and I stood before my court dressed in too cute bebe gear (courtesy of the five finger discount), tellin' an itty bitty white lie about meeting Haneef backstage and how he was checking for me, er'body and their mama's mama believed it. All except, of course, the hater, Ciera.

We were standing at the bus stop waiting for the bus to come.

"Funny," Ciera twisted her lips, while tapping her stiletto heels against the uneven concrete. "I didn't see you backstage and I know this for a fact 'cause I was there." She pointed to her choir of flunkies, who backed her up with a buncha "Uhmm hmmms."

I glared at Ciera—I wanted to catch this chick in the throat. "You should really stop hatin', 'fore we tell everybody how you went backstage, spun around, and became Superhead."

Naja sucked in her inner checks and made a face like Nemo, causing Ciera's neck swerve to kick into overdrive. "You tryna play me?!" Ciera screamed. "Let me tell you something—" and she threw her shoulders back in her get-it-poppin' mode.

"Tell us what?!" Naja cut her off and instantly an argument ensued. The girls standing around egged us on. Yet strangely enough, their instigating turned into outright screaming, and them wildly jumping up and down. I couldn't believe they were being so extra!

"What the hell is y'all's problem?!" I asked. "And you, Samantha," I said, and pointed to one of the girls from my homeroom class, "I'm real surprised that you frontin'—"

"Ha-ha-ha—" Samantha sputtered.

"And you laughin' in my face!"

"Li'l Ma, what's good? I missed you last night." A smooth and familiar male voice floated over my shoulder from nowhere, but I was too amped to acknowledge it. Besides, he couldn't have been talkin to me.

"And another thing—" I said as I felt a strong arm wrap around my waist, stopping me dead in my tracks.

I brushed the arm from my waist and immediately the diamond link bracelet that draped down the caramel colored male forearm caught my attention.

I stood frozen. I didn't know who the hell this was. But I knew it wasn't Jahaad. His broke ass couldn't afford no real bling.

I turned around to see exactly who I needed to cuss out for putting their hands on me, but before the words could fall from my mouth, I started screaming and hugging my future baby daddy tightly. "Haneef!!!! Oh, my God . . . oh, my God."

Oxygen. I needed oxygen. I fanned my face and then turned to Naja, who was holding her chest and puffing into a brown paper bag.

"Wassup, Li'l Ma?" Haneef said. "I missed you."

I couldn't believe this. I had to hug him again.

"You missed me?" Haneef asked.

"Yes." I was in shock, so I'm not even sure if I said that out loud.

"Yeah?" he smiled . . . and oh, what a beautiful smile. "Li'l Ma—"

I put my hand up for him to stop. It was too much to digest at once. I thought I heard him say, "Li'l Ma." That was the sexiest goddamn Li'l Ma I'd ever heard in my life! For once, it was really all good in the hood! I took a deep breath and said slowly, especially since I was on the verge of passing out, "Yes, Daddy?" I knew I sounded pathetic. But . . . whatever . . .

"I don't mind you hugging me, baby."

I swore he called me baby? I hugged him tighter and stomped my feet. Had . . . he . . . just . . . called me . . . baby?!

"But you a little too up in my chest wit' it," he continued. "And I can't breathe."

Oh, I guess I was holding him kind of close. I let him go but I didn't move back, not one inch.

"Now, peep this," l'il tender said. "I wanna hollah at you for a minute. Come take a ride with me."

Just then, the air froze and time stood still. I realized I was dreaming. I looked back at Naja, who was still breathing into the paper bag. "I think I'm dreaming."

"Me, too," she said. "But I ain't waking up."

I turned back to Haneef and blinked. He couldn't be real. Yeah, that was it, he wasn't real. As a matter of fact, he had to be an imposter. I was betting this was somebody Jahaad tricked all his li'l minimum wage Burger King money on to fool me.

I squinted my eyes at who I had just decided was an imposter and said, "I should punch you in the damn face for fakin' the funk!"

"What?" he stepped back.

"You ain't Haneef," I snapped.

"That's Haneef," Naja insisted.

"How do you know?!" I spat.

"I can look at his booty and tell."

"Hmph . . . good point . . ." I paused, turned around and looked at the driver standing outside of the crisp and gleaming black Hummer, holding open the back door. Then I looked at the two men, standing outside of the Lincoln town car, parked in front of the Hummer. They were so buff, they were either bodyguards, or hit men . . . So, maybe . . . maybe . . . this was . . . nope, I was trippin'.

This was the hood; mofos don't just appear around here, unless they're filming a gangsta movie. So obviously, this was some bullshit. Somebody tryna be funny. I looked at whoever this was and wondered if I should let him pull this off, or cold-cock 'im in the face.

"You ai'ight, Li'l Ma?"

I wanted God to stop playing before I really started to think this was Haneef. I sized him up with my eyes: six feet—check. Tattoo of his name on the right side of his neck—check.

Jeeeeeeee'sussssssss! This *was* Haneef. Okay, okay . . . I had to calm down. I was gonna let the other birds go wild, but I had to get it together. After all, he was a nineteen-year-old boy. A boy?! There I was trippin' again; this was a man. A grown ass man. One fine specimen of a man . . .

"What you got, a boyfriend or something, Li'l Ma?" Haneef asked.

Immediately that captured my attention. "What?

Boy, don't play with me." Hell, at that moment, Jahaad didn't count.

"Cool," he pointed toward his Hummer. "So, can we chill?" he asked as the crowd grew and the screams escalated.

I turned around, smiled at Naja, who was fanning her face, and mouthed to Ciera, "Hater." I turned to Haneef and said as cool and calm as melting ice, "Yeah, we can chill."

I eased into the backseat, closed my eyes, and said a quick prayer. "Okay God, if this is a dream, don't bother me with reality."

SPIN IT . . .

Track 7

As we entered the highway and blended into rush hour traffic, I thought of something: Suppose this cat was a stalker? I was so busy getting my groupie on that I didn't even think about why this dude was showing up at my school, anxious to take me around in his Hummer like I was Kim Porter, Maneka, or one of them type chicks.

I turned to him. "You know my mama gon' be lookin' for me." I knew that was a lie, but heck, he didn't have to know that. The butterflies in my stomach were killing me. I was so nervous, I was certain the words "sweatin' like hell" were encrypted on my forehead.

Haneef laughed and flipped open his cell phone, "You wanna call her?"

I couldn't help but blush. "Boy, I'm grown."

He laughed again. "Ai'ight, since you're grown and everything." He arched his eyebrows.

"So, ahhhh . . . " I said as we got on the New Jersey Turnpike heading toward the Holland Tunnel. "Why are you doing all of this?"

"I'm always anxious to please a fan, especially since I didn't see you backstage last night. I wanted to come hollah at you, and tell you that you killed it out there."

"Thank you," I swallowed, scared to look him in the eyes.

Maybe he wanted me to be his protégée. Or perhaps this was a publicity stunt . . . or an offer for a record deal. Or both.

But then again . . . maybe he found out I was a crackhead's kid, felt sorry for me, and has a TV camera following us around. I turned and looked out both the back windows.

"What are you looking for?" he asked.

"Any news crews following us around?"

"News?" he looked out of both windows. "Why, you see somebody? I hope not, but I wouldn't be surprised."

"No, I don't see anyone."

"So why did you ask?"

"Just askin'."

"Ai'ight . . . so what happened to you coming backstage last night?"

My heart was skipping beats. "Uhmmmm, my sister . . . was sick. And I needed to leave."

"Really? Where was ya moms? At work?"

I stared at him. She was at work alright. "Yeah. At work, and she couldn't take off." I was very uncomfortable, but after a few moments, we pulled up to a New York pier, where there was a small boat waiting at the docks. I couldn't believe it. A real boat.

I slyly pinched my right thigh to see if the moment was real, and when I felt pain, I realized nothing had changed and it was actually happening to me.

The water was amazing and the evening sun was turning crimson and leaving illuminated shadows across the ripples. I was speechless. I got out of the car, took his hand, and got on the boat. Was this what the rich and famous did? Ride boats all day? Dang, this was the life.

Haneef smiled at the captain. "Wassup? Elite, this is Kool-Out, my thugged-out captain," he laughed.

"Funny, sir," the captain said.

Did he just call him sir?

"Nawl, I'm buggin'. This is John," Haneef said. "He's going to drive us around tonight."

"Pleased to make your acquaintance, madam."

Madam? Not knowing what to do, I smiled and watched him return to the captain's booth a few steps below, leaving Haneef and I on the main deck all alone. "Sit down," Haneef said as he pointed to a reclining chair, but for some reason I continued to stand, even as we pulled into the open sea.

"I hope you like cheeseburgers and sweet potato fries." Haneef smiled and pointed to the table in the center of the deck, which was dressed with silver domes. He lifted them and revealed the menu he'd just described.

Hmph, I could've sworn this dude was trying to get with me. But that wasn't going to happen. After all, he already said this was about pleasing a fan. So, I was going to keep it movin'.

"Wow, this looks delicious," I said as we sat down to eat, still looking over my shoulder for an unexpected news crew.

After we ate dinner, I was too nervous to be myself, so I decided to play the nice and quiet type.

"Have you ever been on a boat?" Haneef asked, cutting across my thoughts.

I laughed. "Uhmmm, yeah."

He stared at me for a moment.

Was I supposed to say more than that?

"Oh . . . kay, when?" he pried.

Is he tryna hold a conversation? "Uhmmmmm . . . okay," I said, answering his question. Remembering the last time I was on a boat, I cracked up laughing. "Last winter there was a blizzard, and these dudes around my way stole a canoe and we went riding up and down the block in it. We had broomsticks for rowing, and the whole nine."

Haneef looked at me like I was crazy.

Maybe I shouldn't have told him that story. He probably thinks I'm ghetto as hell. "I guess that was a li'l ghetto, huh?" I asked.

"A little? A whole lot," he laughed. "But I got a story to top that."

I twisted my lips. "What?"

"Ai'ight, check it." He draped his arm behind my seat. "When we lived in Baltimore, my older brother, Khalil, bought a school bus, had the top taken off, took the seats out, and made it a pool."

"Oh, no!" I cracked up. "Say, word?"

"Word. Li'l Ma, we swam in that pool all summer. We were straight coolin'."

"That sounds like something my brother, Ny'eem, would do."

"How many brothers and sisters do you have?" he stroked my hair to the back.

"Two brothers and two sisters. I'm the oldest and my sisters are twins. And you?"

"All brothers and I'm the youngest."

"Yeah?"

"Yeah, it's five of us."

"What? It's five of us," I said, a little too excited.

"You like having a big family?"

"Not really," I said. "If I wasn't the oldest, maybe it wouldn't be so bad."

"Why?"

"Because then I wouldn't have to take care of everything and everybody."

"You take care of everything and everybody? Why?"

I paused. I was becoming a little too comfortable. "No reason. My mother just works all the time."

"Where's your dad?"

"Dead," I said too quickly for him not to think I

was lying, so I changed the subject. "Your concert was the truth," I smiled. "Word up, you did your thing."

"You, too, Li'l Ma. You looked soooooo pretty out there. And when you started singing, did you hear the crowd go wild? You got talent, Li'l Ma, for real."

Was Haneef sayin' I had talent? I believe he was. "Thank you," I blushed.

"How long have you been singing?" he asked me.

"Since I was five." I told him the story of how I would sing all the time, skipping the times and leaving out stories of how my mother had me singing for drug dealers so she could get drugs. And before I knew it, we were kicking it like old friends. Like he was just a regular ole dude. And I couldn't believe it. He made me feel so comfortable that home seemed a world away.

This was crazy. Not only was I with the number one hip-hop sensation, but I was chillin' with him. Kickin' it. Laughing and talking. Exchanging stories like it could possibly go further than this moment, or further than tonight, but knowing for sure that things in my life never worked out like that. So I took it for what it was worth and enjoyed—whatever this was.

Haneef cut on the radio and the commercial for the radio contest was playing the winning song I sang, stopping right before my mother wrecked my life on the phone. "Listen at you, girl. And here I thought I was hot."

I rolled my eyes to the sky. "Sweat yourself, why don't you?!" I joked . . . I hoped I didn't sound stupid.

"You really wrote that song you were singing?"

Out of embarrassment, I held my head down. "Yes."

He lifted my chin. "That was beautiful."

"Thank you."

Haneef smiled and pulled me softly to his chest. "Yo, you know what I want you to do?" he said as we started to slow dance to the music playing on the radio.

"What?"

"When you drop your first CD, I want you to write a song and dedicate it to me."

I cracked up. "And call it what?"

"Love Letter," he laughed. "What else? And be like this is for my boo, Haneef."

Was he serious? "My boo?" I said, taken aback. "Uhmmm, I'ma be like this is to please a fan."

"A fan?" he frowned, as we continued to dance.

"Yeah, a fan."

After a few moments of silence, he said, "I want you to sing to me."

My eyes lit up with such delight, there were no words to describe how I felt. There I was with the man of my dreams in the middle of the sea, and he wanted to dance with me. He placed his hands around my waist and I locked my fingers around his neck and looked directly in his eyes.

The moon shone on us like a spotlight as we swayed back and forth. I was in heaven.

"You have a beautiful voice," he insisted. "And I would love to hear it again."

I swallowed, took a deep breath, closed my eyes, followed the melody floating around in my head, and sang about this being more than just a silly crush.

After the song ended, he said, "That was hot." He stared at me and slowly our lips drew toward one another, but just at the moment, my cell phone rang.

I thought about ignoring it, but I knew from the ringtone it was someone from my house. And since I hadn't been home since that morning, I figured I needed to get it.

I stepped away from him and flipped open my phone. It was Aniyah. There was so much static I could barely make out what she was saying, but the only thing that came through clearly was how everybody in the house, once again, was dead.

"Alright, Aniyah." I closed my phone and looked at Haneef.

"You need to bounce?" he asked me.

"Yeah," I said. "I need to get back."

He walked into the captain's booth, and before I knew it, the boat was turning around. And I was doing everything in my power not to let the tears bubbling up in my eyes run down my cheeks.

SPIN IT . . .

Track 8

"Okay, and why couldn't I get at you all last night?!" Naja said as soon as I walked into school, pulling me by my arm away from the other students who were dying to know what the heck I was doing with Haneef yesterday. "And why didn't you meet me at the bus stop this morning?" she carried on. "And what did he say, and what did he do?" she rambled, not taking a breath. "Girl, it's a good thing you always around here lookin' cute. You gon' see him today? You think he could break up Chris Brown and Rihanna? What you think Chris Brown's real name is, Richard? Oh, I don't care. Just give me the four-one-one—"

Richard? "Anyway," I said, as we stood in front of my locker, "let me tell you this. Haneef took me to New York."

"New York?" she froze. "New York City? Like the

place where the Statue of Liberty is? The Big Grape—"

"It's the Big Apple."

"Whatever. So what did y'all do? You didn't give him any, did you? Please don't tell me you hit him off like a nightly fruit stand—"

"It's one-night stand."

"Dang, Elite," she said, disappointed. "That's even worse."

"No. That's not what I meant—"

"Did you give him some booty?"

"No. I'm not a ho."

"Ai'ight then. Why didn't you say that?"

"Oh . . . my . . . God . . . would you just listen?!"

"I'm listening. What's the problem?"

I took a deep breath. "We chilled on his boat. He had dinner prepared and everything."

"Get outta here!" she said breathlessly, holding her chest. "That is so romantic."

"Yes, girl, in the middle of the sea."

"Under the moonlight?"

"Yes," I said breathlessly.

We both fell against the lockers.

"I'm in love," we said simultaneously.

"You know what I mean," Naja snapped. "Any-who, go on."

"Gurl," I said as I closed my eyes tightly. I swear I was still high off the moment. "It was the best."

"Did you kiss him?"

"Almost."

"Almost?" she frowned. "Almost doesn't count."

"I know, but Aniyah bum-rushed my flow—she called and said everybody was dead."

"Damn, what, they die every other night? Did you ever think about calling the Book of World Records? Cause my granddaddy only died once." She tapped her acrylic nailtip on her bottom lip. "Unless he came back and bounced. Cause he couldn't stand Mom-Mom."

Sometimes I wondered how in the world we were best friends.

"So anyway," she said. "Get to the good part. Are you two an item?"

"An item?" I wrinkled my nose.

"Yeah, is that your boo?"

"No," I shook my head. "He's not my boo and honestly," I sighed, "I don't think he's feeling me like that."

"And why not?"

"Because when I asked him what all of this was for, he said he was always eager 'to please a fan.'"

"A fan? He was all up in yo' grill, and he's reduced you to being a—fan?"

"I don't know if I would call it being reduced."

"Well, what the hell you think it is? He damn near called you a played-out groupie. A fan—"

"Naja—"

"Here this cat stole your information—"

"Stole—?"

"Stole it, and he stalked you—"

"Stalked—?"

"Stalked you. Stalked the hell outta you, and then he turns around after sailing you all around the Chinese Apple—"

"It's the Big Apple—just the Big Apple—"

"Work with me now—you know what I mean—he done row-row-rowed ya boat down the Big Apple's stream, and now you a fan? And you taking that? Girl, call that cat so I can check his chin like a four-hour short stay."

I hated it when she had a point. Before I commented on how played I suddenly felt, the morning bell rang and it was time to head to homeroom. "I'll catch you at lunchtime," Naja said as she headed down the opposite end of the hallway.

I grabbed my books from my locker, slammed it shut, and headed down the hall toward my class. As soon as I turned the corner, I was jerked back and tossed against my locker. It was Jahaad. I snatched my left forearm from his grip. "What are you doing?!" This fool was trippin'. I went to move and he pushed me back.

"Boy," I squinted, "don't play with me! You know I don't go for nobody putting their hands on me!"

"What you call yourself doing yesterday, huh?" He was so close to my face, the warmth of his breath smothered my nose. "You went home with that dude? You a groupie ass ho now?!"

"You better get out my face!"

"I don't better do nothin', but you better explain yourself to me! You know how that made me look?! Do you know what that did to my reputation around here?!"

I couldn't believe this—this nucka here had lost his mind. "You got a lot of nerve when you been off galavantin' with Ceira's ho ass!"

"I ain't with Ciera. I'm with you!"

"Stop lying. I was right there next to her in the mall the other day when you called her on the phone, right after you called me on mine! You ain't slick!"

"I only called Ciera once, and that was to get the homework. So what's your excuse?"

"Boy, you need to stop lyin'! She's not even in any of your classes."

"She is so! And anyway, back to the subject at hand. I can't believe you would do me like this, Elite! After everything I've done for you?! After I've always been there for you, you skip off with some rap dude?"

"He's not a rapper, and I didn't exactly skip off with him."

"Now you need to stop lying."

"Well we didn't skip, we were in a car."

"You being funny?"

I sucked my teeth. "Look . . ." I paused. I had to think of how I would finish this lie. "Him coming here was a part of the radio contest." Yeah, that was it, the radio contest. "And he met me here. I took a limo ride with him and nothing else. He did it to please a fan. I don't even think he remembers my name."

"For real?" Jahaad smiled.

"On the really real." That was pathetic. I couldn't believe he bought that.

"I told you all those type cats do is use chicks."

"I know," I pacified him.

"I know you do. Now tell me you still love me?"

"You know I do." He was making me sick.

"Ai'ight, so why don't you come to my house after school and prove it."

I was guessing Jahaad missed the memo, but having sex with him was out. He didn't like to use condoms and I wasn't passing off anymore without them. After my pregnancy scare a few months back, there was no way I was going to take the chance. Not to mention, I had this sneaky suspicion that he was really doin' ole girl Ciera. And if so, he could forget it, 'cause there was no way I was droppin' it behind no ho. "I gotta work after school, Jahaad. So I'll call you, but right now I have to get to class."

"Yeah, ai'ight." He stepped from in front of me. "Get to class." I know he was pissed, but so what? I had other things to do than babysit his insecurities by giving him some unprotected booty.

SPIN IT . . .

Track 9

"Hold up! Wait a minute!" Samantha screamed across the cafeteria like she'd lost every bit of her mind. Naja and I held our lunch trays in our hands, stunned.

"She can't be talking to us," I said as I shook my head and turned to Naja.

"Nah, I don't think she is because she knows I don't get down with her like that."

"For real, though," I said and we continued walking.

"Elite! Naja! I know y'all hear me!" Samantha screamed again.

"She is talking to us," I said in disbelief.

"That trick is trippin'." We turned toward Samantha.

"Ahnt aunnn, come over here!" came from another direction. We spun back around. And it was

Mecca—from my math class. The same Mecca who's never said more than two words to me—yet she was motioning for us to sit at the table with her and her posse. Uhm, not.

Instead of walking toward Mecca or Samantha, we headed toward an empty table in the cut.

"Told y'all she was a ho," Ciera said as she brushed past me. "Now everybody on her 'cause she givin' it up to that played-out Haneef. I heard he lip-syncs anyway."

I whipped around and spat at her, "I heard you were really a man, and what? Now you got something else you wanna say to me?"

Ciera wiggled her neck. "I know you didn't just call me a man."

"I sure did, Henry," I snapped sarcastically.

"Whatever," she flicked her hand.

"Yeah, whatever," I said as we continued on our way. "Stank ass trick."

"Forget her," Samantha said, pulling me by my arm.

"Yeah," Mecca chimed in. "First period lunch is only forty-five minutes, so you don't have time to be arguing with her."

"Exactly," Samantha agreed. "We need to hear what went on with you and Haneef."

We sat our lunch trays on the table and a smile ran across my face.

"They were on a yacht," Naja said before I could open my mouth.

"Well we weren't exactly—"

She kicked me under the table. "After he flew her to California—Beverly Hills to be exact," Naja spat.

"Beverly Hills?" All the girls gasped. "Oh, my."

"He told her it was love at first sight."

"He did, Elite?" Samantha's mouth gaped open.

"Yeah," I added to the truth's remix, "he did. I was in heaven."

"Somebody said he told you—you could quit school and he would take care of you," Mecca said as a few girls I'd seen around school joined us.

"He did tell her that," Naja said.

"But I told him I didn't want to do that," I interjected.

"But I heard he was going with that new singer, Deidra."

"She's a tramp," Naja spat.

"She sure is," I added. "Besides, he dumped her."

"He did?" a few of them asked.

"Yop," I shook my head in assurance. "Sho' did."

"Dang!" was their response.

"But what about Jahaad?" Tiffany, another girl who'd joined us, asked.

"What he don't know—" I spat.

"Won't hurt him," Naja added.

"Fa'sho," Samantha laughed as the lunch bell rang.

We all got up from the table and Naja and I continued to brag as we walked into the hallway toward class, where we saw Jahaad and a few of his boys coming our way.

"Shhhh . . ." Samantha said. "Here comes ole boy."

Instantly we were silent, but the moment Jahaad and his crew walked past us, we screamed in laughter. We didn't dare turn around because we knew they were looking at us like we we'd lost our minds.

"Ai'ight," Samantha said. "Elite, call me."

She wanted me to call her? I didn't even have her number. I knew we just bugged out in the caf, but she couldn't be serious. "Okay, girl." I waved bye.

"Bye, Elite," Mecca waved. "Wait for me after school. I'ma take the bus with you."

"Dang, girl," Naja said. "Before long, you ain't gon' have time for me."

"Please," I said and mushed her playfully on the side of her head. "I'ma always have time for you, big head." And we went our separate ways to class.

SPIN IT . . .

Track 10

I had a week's worth of clothes I needed to sneak back into the boutique but that night it seemed like Thelma just wouldn't leave. Naja was off so there wasn't much I could do to distract my manager. I twiddled my thumbs hoping she would get lost, but after an hour of seeing how she wouldn't bounce, I realized I was walking around with a backpack filled with stolen merchandise. This was a hot ass mess.

In between thoughts of how I was gonna sneak back the clothes where they belonged, I thought about calling Haneef, but quickly changed my mind. After all, it had been a week since we sailed the ocean blue and I hadn't heard from him. Not once. So I figured forget him. Yeah, that was it. I had to forget him.

There weren't many customers in the store so I

was able to finish all my homework. "Elite," Thelma caught my attention. "I'm leaving early."

I was thanking God. "Awwl, Thelma. Why?"

"Because there's not much action in here, and I don't feel too well. So I'll see you tomorrow after school."

"Okay," I said as I watched her walk toward the door.

I waited a few minutes to be sure she was gone, and then I took out the clothes from my backpack and laid them on the counter. I ran in the back quickly, grabbed a stack of hangers, and when I came back out, Thelma was looking at the clothes on the counter.

"Where did these come from?" she asked.

"Uhmm . . . a customer," I said, and paused, "who . . . just went to the bathroom and said she'd be returning these."

"Okay, well be sure she has the receipt."

"Okay," I tried to play off my nervousness. "I will."

"I'm gone this time for sure," she said, heading out the door, and when she was out of sight, I let out the longest sigh in the world. That was it for "borrowing" clothes!

I returned to the cash register and my phone rang. I looked at the caller ID, and it was Jahaad. I really wasn't feeling him since he pulled that stunt at school last week, but I answered anyway. "Hello?"

"Wassup, boo? Where you at?"

"Work."

"Let me come scoop you."

I looked at the clock and thought about how I really needed my money to stretch until the next week, when I would be able to afford a new bus card. "Ai'ight," I said. "Come get me in an hour."

As the hour passed I did the books, set up the schedule, and placed some of the new merchandise on the floor. By closing time I'd made sure the clothes I'd returned were in their proper place, locked up the store, dropped the money in the vault, and when I walked outside, Jahaad was sitting in his car.

"You know my mother's not home tonight," he said before I even closed the door. "So you could spend the night like you used to."

"No, thank you," I snapped.

"And why not?"

I shrugged my shoulders, "Cause I said no."

"And I said why?"

"Look, you not gettin' no booty. Now take me home, please."

"I don't believe you frontin' on me."

"Believe it. Now can you drive?"

"Nah, I don't think that's a good idea."

"So what you tryna say? That you ain't taking me home?"

"I'm tryna say that if you ain't passin' off, then maybe you should take the bus home."

"What?" I couldn't believe this.

"Yeah." And he shook his head to confirm what he'd just said. "Yeah. Matter a fact, here comes the bus now."

I couldn't believe this. I had absolutely no words for him. "You know we through then, right Jahaad?" I snapped.

"Yeah," he said as I slammed the door behind me. "Pretty much."

By the time I got home, the shock of what Jahaad had pulled on me had formed into tears. I walked in my door but before I could close it and decide where I could find a quiet spot in the house to cry, the twins and Mica ran toward me. "Elite!" I looked down and they were crying. "I'm glad you're home."

"What's wrong?" I panicked.

"Mommy and Gary—" Aniyah pointed—"are tearing up the house looking for money."

"Where the hell is my money, Elite?" My mother stormed in the room toward me.

"What are you talking about?" I frowned at her. She was wild in the eyes, and I'd never seen her look this way. I could tell she was high, but she'd never been high quite like this before. For a moment I wondered if she was doing something other than crack. I looked at my sisters and brother. "Y'all go in the other room!"

"Don't tell my damn kids what to do! These are my kids and I'm the mama around here. Now where the hell is my money?"

"What money?"

"My welfare money. My Work First card has a zero balance."

"I paid the rent with it!"

My mother raised her hand and slapped me so hard I stumbled directly into Jahaad, who was at the front door. "Let me tell you something," my mother spat. "Don't you ever take my money! You understand me?" She snatched my purse from me and emptied the contents on the floor.

"Wooooo," Jahaad said, walking into the apartment. "Wait—wait, Ms. Parker." He went in his wallet. "How much you need?" He pulled out a hundred dollar bill. "Here, take this."

"Jahaad," I said, wiping my tears and fighting off my embarrassment. "You don't need to do that."

"It's okay." He looked at me with pity in his eyes. "I'm straight."

My mother snatched the money from his hands, and she and Gary disappeared out the door. I didn't even know what to say. "Jahaad—I'm sorry—"

"Look," he said as he stroked my cheek, "you didn't do anything. If anything, I should be apologizing to you. My fault for what I did tonight. That was foul—real foul—and I hope you forgive me."

Now that was the Jahaad I remembered, and all I could do was hug him. "I forgive you," I said, knowing that despite him giving my mother money and getting her off me, my feelings for him were fading.

After a few hours of Jahaad sitting with me and us planning a future that I felt like both of us were questioning the validity of, Sydney walked into the living room. "Elite," she said in the loudest whisper in the world. "I gotta tell you a secret."

"A what?"

"A secret. Some dude named Haneef called and Aniyah told me to whisper it in your ear. So, can you come over here so I can tell you?"

I swallowed because I felt the heat from Jahaad's eyes piercing through me. "Don't worry, Sydney, you just told me."

SPIN IT . . .

Track 11

The hundred dollars and that Haneef was my rich and rappin' jump-off was thrown at me constantly after that. Jahaad just kept tossing it in my face.

Along with that, after Haneef came to school and picked me up, I had more chicks either trying to be my friend or thinking they could talk about me and spread rumors like wildfire: I was a ho, I was going with both Jahaad and Haneef, I thought I was cute . . . (well, maybe the "I thought I was cute" part was true, but still), that I gave it up to Haneef on the first date, and on and on it went.

And what was funny was that none of them knew my real life story, and that the version I'd sold them was straight fiction. I told them my dad was in the army and stationed in Iraq, and that my mother was a nurse, though I told the truth about my brothers and sisters. There was no way I was gonna deny their existence, even if I'd wanted to.

I lay back on my bed and stared at the ceiling, wondering what it would be like to be famous and if I could really be like Mary J. or Keyshia Cole. Then maybe I'd be able to pay for my mother to go to rehab, buy us a house with a pool in the backyard, and then maybe . . . I would even fix up this place so whoever came in here after us would feel some hope, and not our despair.

"Elite!" Ny'eem called, opening my bedroom door at the same time.

"Wassup?" I sat up and looked at him.

"I'ma take the twins and Mica to the movies."

I couldn't believe it. "What? You? Is it a storm outside?" I laughed.

"Funny."

"But nah, I just felt like chillin' with them."

"You need some money?"

"Nah, I got it."

"Bus fare?"

"What did I just tell you?"

"Snacks?"

"No," and he closed the door behind him. But then I got up and went into the living room. I was happy he was taking them somewhere, but I had to make sure they looked decent. And wouldn't you know it, as soon as I stepped into the living room, Mica had a sheet wrapped around his neck and the twins looked a hot ass mess with my clothes on.

“If you,” I pointed to each of them, “don’t take that mess off, you won’t be going anywhere!”

“What’s wrong with ’em?” Ny’eem asked.

“Mica looks like a jacked Superman, and the twins, don’t they look crazy to you? Ny’eem, you’re not dressing like that.”

“Don’t compare me to no li’l kids, ai’ight? I’ma grown ass man, dawg, and besides, I thought they looked kinda fly.”

“What? Boy, don’t play with me.” I balled up my fist. “Now, bounce.” I pointed back at Mica and the twins. “In your room and change your clothes.”

Reluctantly, and with the biggest attitudes in the world, they went in the other room and redressed. A few minutes later they came out looking like someone took care of them. I kissed them all on the foreheads and said, “Now you look real cute.”

“Uhmm hmm,” the twins twisted their lips to the side.

“Can we go now, Mother?” Ny’eem asked sarcastically.

“Yes, son,” I replied with the same sarcasm. “Now you can leave.”

“Always think she’s somebody’s mother,” Sydney mumbled under her breath.

“What you say, Syd?” I snapped.

“Nothing.”

Mica looked at me. “She said—”

“Say it,” Sydney threatened, “and see if that sheet you wrap yourself in don’t disappear.”

"She said—" Mica gave me a toothless and nervous grin—"that you look real pretty." And then he waved bye and smiled as they proceeded out the door.

A few minutes later, I thought better about not giving Ny'eem any money, and that I'd slide twenty dollars in Aniyah or Sydney's pocket, just in case . . . whatever just in case was.

"Wait!" I ran out the door and tried to catch up to them. But as I got to the front door of the building, they were nowhere in sight. "Dang!"

"Elite," I heard a whisper float in my direction. "Elite."

I looked down and it was my mother's boyfriend, Gary, crouched in the corner, with a lit cigarette shaking from the corner of his mouth. "Yo, let me hollah at you for a minute."

"Ill, you better go hollah at a job and get the hell out my face!"

"I got a job. That's what I wanna talk to you about. You think you could loan me two dollars and twenty-seven cents so I can get back and forth to work next week?"

"Two dollars and twenty-seven cents? How did you even come up with that? Man, please." I couldn't believe it. Now Gary was asking me for money? "I can't believe you're asking me for money!"

"What did he ask you?!" My mother stormed toward us, crossing the street to the front of the building.

"Where did you come from?" Gary stood up nervously. "I was just getting to know my daughter."

"Your daughter?! Ill. Not." I frowned. My daddy might have been a scumbag, but he wasn't this scumbag.

My mother looked at Gary as if she could've sliced his throat. "These is not yo' kids, Gary. You done gone crazy? Now," she looked at me, "what the hell did he ask you?"

"For two dollars and twenty-seven cents," I snapped.

"You asked my baby for some money?!" My mother started screaming, and the next thing I knew it was a full-fledged fallout. They were cussing and carrying on in the street, and the only words I could make out were, "How you gon' ask my child for two dollars? You ain't me!"

That was my cue. Her bein' extra with Gary must've been a weak attempt at an apology.

Whatever.

I ran back inside the apartment, grabbed my purse, and made sure the doors were all locked. Then I proceeded down the block to Naja's house.

Ten minutes later, I rang Naja's bell and her grandmother came to the door. She stared at me like she could've slapped me into next week. "I know damn well you didn't come to church dressed like that?!"

"Church?" I said, taken aback.

"Yeah, church," she snapped. "God's crib."

Oh . . . kay . . .

I didn't know whether to go in or to leave, so I stood in the doorway before deciding what to do. "Naja!" I yelled.

She came running from the back. "Girl, what are you yelling for? The bell works."

"Mom-Mom—" I pointed.

"It's Sister Delicious," Mom-Mom snapped. "Didn't I just tell you it was Sunday?"

"Ma!" Naja yelled as she walked to the door and I stepped in.

"What is it?" Neecy responded.

"Come get Mom-Mom."

Neecy walked into the living room wearing a robe and rollers in her hair.

"Oh . . . my . . . God," Mom-Mom said. "I know damn well," she pointed at the TV screen with Creflo Dollar on full blast, "you ain't come in here amongst all these church folk dressed like a tramp. I told my son you was a heathen."

"Oh . . . kay . . ." I mumbled to myself, wondering why I'd left my own house.

"Mom-Mom," Neecy said as she grabbed her hand, "Oprah is looking for you."

Oprah?

"I don't speak to Oprah no more," Mom-Mom said. "Not after she stole Stedman from me."

And I thought my house was live.

Naja and I walked to her room and she cut the radio and TV on. We watched some videos and listened to some music, but decided two hours later we were bored as heck.

"So what we gon' do today?" Naja asked.

"I don't know, but there has to be something to do."

"It is Sunday."

"True."

Before I could respond, my phone rang.

I looked at the caller ID. Haneef. "It's Haneef," I panted.

"What? Haneef? Oh, my God!" Naja screamed. "I wonder if you won another radio contest."

"I didn't try for another contest."

"So, you could've still won."

"Huh?"

"Anyway, you gon' answer it?"

"I can't." I tossed the phone to her. "You answer it."

"I can't."

"Why?"

"I might try to get with him. So you better get it, before he hangs up."

"Good point. And I would hate for us to fall out." I flipped open the phone. "Hello?"

"Wassup, Li'l Ma?"

There went that sexy ass Li'l Ma again. "Nothin'. Chillin'." I hoped the forced confidence in my voice made up for the butterflies taking over my belly.

He laughed. "Well, I'm back in town and my CD just went platinum, so I'm having a party. I want you to come and chill with me."

"Me?" I couldn't believe it. "You going a long way just to please a fan, don't you think?"

"That's how I do it, Li'l Ma," he said. "You ai'ight with that?"

"I guess."

"You guess?"

I laughed. "No, it's cool."

"So you comin'?"

"Uhmmm hmmm," was my attempt to keep playing it cool.

"Straight. So meet me around nine o'clock on 165 Grand Street at the Palace Club, and ask for James. He's on my security team and he'll show you to V.I.P."

"Ai'ight."

"Ai'ight, Li'l Ma. One." And he hung up.

"What happened?" Naja asked.

As I went to answer, all that came out of my mouth were screams: "Ahhhhhhhhhhhhhhhhhhhhh!!!!!!!!!!!!!!!!!!!!"

"The choir singin'?" Mom-Mom pounded on Naja's door. "I'm 'spose to sing lead."

"You better tell me what he said right now," Naja snapped, "or I'ma let Delicious in here."

"Okay . . . okay . . . he said, he wanted to go out. To meet him at the Palace around nine."

"Oh hell, yeah, we goin'," Naja insisted.

"We? Don't you have a curfew?"

"What, girl, a body pillow tucked under my sheet does wonders. Plus this is my mother's bingo night. So she'll be gone forever."

"Good!" I said excited, and then I remembered

that I had a few dollars but my money was limited. "How we gon' get there?"

"I'll ask my dad for the car."

"And what we gon' wear?"

She hopped off the bed and ran over to her closet, "Welcome to the world of bebe."

I stood stunned. "You didn't take that back?"

"Heck, no. Did you?"

"Yeah."

"You stupid then. Not I. I'ma rock my gear. And some of it I haven't even wore yet."

"Dang. I don't know about keeping it, Naja. Suppose Thelma gets suspicious."

"Gurl, Thelma can't see her way outta paper bag. She ain't thinking about these clothes."

"I don't know," I said wearily.

"Stop worrying about that and let's get down with the get down, and see what we gon' wear."

After sorting through the clothes, I picked out a fitted black miniskirt and a halter. I had a leather midriff jacket and some stilettos at my house, which I quickly ran to get and hurried back. Now my entire outfit was fiyah. Naja put on a tight denim skirt with a cute backless shirt, a matching leather jacket, and a pair of stilettos. Hot was not the word for how we looked. Fierce was more like it.

Once we were dressed and our hair was flat-ironed straight, Naja said, "Come on. My mother should be gone so I can ask my daddy now."

We went in the living room where her father was watching TV. "Daddy," Naja whined.

"Yup-Yup."

"Can I," she twisted her finger into her dimpled cheek, "borrow the car to go out?"

"Hell, no." Her mother walked into the living room, fully dressed, with her purse tucked under her arm.

"Where did you come from?" Naja asked in shock.

"That doesn't matter. All that matters is no, you cannot borrow the car."

"But why?"

"Because I said so! And besides, you have school tomorrow. Not to mention, you just got your license and you're too young to be driving my car all over the place."

"It's Daddy's car," Naja snapped.

"Oh, you getting smart?!" Neecy said. "Hmph. Well, you really ain't goin' now." Neecey kissed Naja's dad on the cheek and left.

I looked at Naja and she was pissed. I twisted my lips and realized we'd just been shut down. When we walked back into Naja's room, I said, "What the heck we gon' do now?"

"Oh, we goin'." She sucked her teeth.

"And how is that?"

"My daddy goes to bed every night at nine. We'll wait until then, and take the car."

"Take the car? Like steal it?"

"No, borrow it."

"Here we go again."

"What's the problem?"

"I don't wanna steal anymore."

“There you go with the stealing. I just said borrow it.”

“Borrow it, like those clothes you borrowed in your closet? That’s stealing.”

“As long as there’s an option to bring it back, it’s borrowing.”

“And what about when your mother comes home and sees the car is gone?”

“She won’t notice. She’ll think Daddy pulled his car in the garage.”

“Are you sure?”

“Yes. Trust me.”

“Alright, Naja, but yo’ ass is mad sneaky.”

When nine o’clock came, it was like clockwork; her dad went to bed and a few minutes later he was asleep. Naja snuck the keys from his pants pocket and a few seconds later we were on our way, rushing down the street like we’d escaped from someplace.

My heart was beating fast, but Naja acted like an expert.

“Girl,” she said, driving down the block, “we gon’ have a ball.”

“Naja, are you sure we should do this?” I asked as we pulled up to the red light.

“Yeah, girl. It’s all good.”

“Okay . . . Naja, I wanna tell you something.”

“What?”

I sighed. “I lied to Haneef about my real life.”

“You lied?”

"Yeah. The night we went out on his boat, I didn't exactly let him bring me home."

"I knew you gave him some booty. Now what sleazy four-hour stay did you hit?"

"Ill, didn't I tell you I was not about to be a ho? What I'm saying is he didn't drop me off in front of the building where I live."

"So, where'd he take you?"

"I had him drop me off in front of your house."

"My house? Girl, don't mess around and have me going with him, and Mom-Mom tryna get at him on the creep."

I laughed.

"But why'd you do that?" she asked.

"Because, I can't tell him about my mother. Do you know how devastated I would be? I swear, I don't want anyone to know that shit."

"Uhmmmm . . . I don't know, Elite. I think maybe you should've just told him the truth. Either that or go all the way with the lie. You shoulda told him you were Reverend Run's love child—"

"What? Okay, that's enough."

"Or you shoulda told him that Kimora Lee Simmons was yo' mama who gave you up for adoption, and that you were raised by wolves."

"Please shut up. Leave it to you to go too far. Now look, we can't stay all night."

"We'll stay for two hours and then bounce."

"Two hours only."

"Ai'ight. So let's get this on and crackin'."

As the light turned red and the car stopped, we heard someone calling our names. "Elite and Naja!" It was Samantha and Mecca. "Where y'all goin'?" they said as they walked up the block toward the traffic light.

"A party," Naja blurted out. "With Haneef."

My eyes bulged out of my head. I could've choked this chick. She knew we didn't get down with them like that.

"Oh, my God, please let us come," Mecca begged, folding her hands in a prayer position. "Puleeeeeeze."

"Y'all not even dressed," I said, hoping they would take the hint.

"It'll only take me a minute to get dressed. Please." Mecca shook her folded hands.

"Y'all can't go without me!" Samantha spat. "And I'm always fly so I'm going just like this." I looked over at Samantha, who wore a pair of tight black jeans, a black and rhinestone studded tee, and a pair of stilettos.

"Yeah," I said. "Maybe you can get over with that. But I'm not sure if they'll let you in the club."

"So what you saying?" Mecca asked. "You don't want us to go?"

"No," Naja shook her head. "She's not saying that. Y'all can come." She elbowed me on the sly.

This was a hot ass mess. Stevie Wonder could see this was a bad idea. We didn't do these birds close enough to be partying with them, let alone partying with them in New York—and with a stolen car at that. But I decided I wasn't gon' even stress. Whatever.

The party leeches got in the backseat and Naja drove to Mecca's house.

"Loosen up," Naja mumbled under her breath.

I didn't even respond.

"And don't be too long," Naja said as we pulled in front of Mecca's house. "We have to hurry up."

A few minutes later Mecca returned, dressed in a pair of glued-on jeans, a super tight tank top, and stilettos. All I could think of was one hot ass mess. I was already embarrassed. And when I looked her over again, I realized she had her oldest sister, Tamara, in tow.

Mecca ducked her head through the passenger window and looked toward Naja. "Tamara wanna know if she can come?" She pointed back to Tamara, and Tamara smiled.

"I wanna chill wit' y'all," Tamara said, sounding pathetic. I knew right then that everything I'd ever heard about this pigeon had to be true. Why else would she wanna hang out with a group of seventeen-year-olds when she was twenty-two? Or was it just me?

"It's not enough room," I said. "Maybe next time."

"She can squeeze between us," Samantha put her two cents in.

"Yeah, I guess," Naja said, sounding reluctant.

The car was extra tight and extra amped as we

drove to New York. I was trying to loosen up, but I was nervous going to meet Haneef. And it wasn't because he was a celebrity. It was more than that. It was like the way you feel when you first meet a dude you realize you not only have a crush on, but he might have a bigger one on you. As a matter of fact, it felt better than that.

My stomach did flips as we zoomed through the Holland Tunnel and passed the sign that read, "Welcome to New York."

Once we found the club, we parked on a dark side street.

"Okay," I said, turning around in my seat. "How do I look?"

"You look fly," Naja said, and the rest of the girls agreed. "Just put on a little more lipstick."

"Oh, okay."

"And how do I look?" Naja looked in the rear-view mirror and fixed her hair.

"Cute," Samantha told her. "You know, we all look fly."

"For real, though," Tamara said.

"Oh," Mecca whispered. "Y'all know what I meant to tell you?"

"What?" Naja whispered.

"And why are y'all whispering?" Samantha asked.

"Oh, my fault," Mecca said. "I know you and Charise cool and all."

"Who's cool with Charise?" Naja rolled her eyes. "I mean she ai'ight, but she ain't my girl."

"Well that's good to hear," Mecca twisted her lips. "Cause she was talkin' 'bout you two like a dog."

"Excuse me?" I batted my eyes.

"Uhmm hmmm," Samantha chimed in. "I do remember hearing something about her sayin' y'all was hos."

"Yup, remember that?" Tamara said. "And she said that when she was sitting on our porch."

"Fa'sho." Mecca snapped her neck from side to side. "She said y'all wasn't nothin' but a buncha groupies."

"And liars."

"What?" I couldn't believe it.

"No, she didn't," Naja said in disbelief.

"Yes, she did," Tamara added.

"But you know I got yo' back," Mecca said. "And I told her she needed to shut up, cause she didn't know what she was running her mouth about."

"You know she a hater," Samantha snapped.

"Wait 'til I see her ass," Naja said.

"She can forget about saying anything else to me," I added.

"Hmph. She's the one that encouraged Ciera to go after Jahaad," Samantha pointed her finger.

"She did what?!" I screeched.

"What you care? You got like . . ." Mecca said, "the black president, sweatin' you."

"So," Naja interrupted. "That was still her boo."

"True. So now you know not to even fool with

that trick." Tamara opened her car door. "Now that that's settled, can we bounce?"

"Yeah, forget her," Samantha seconded the motion. "We gotta party to attend."

And we stepped like five top models down the Paris runway as we walked toward the club, only to see that the entrance line was wrapped around the block.

"What in the . . ." I said as my mouth dropped open.

"Dang, this line is gon' take forever."

"Line? I thought you had an in with Haneef!" Mecca spat. "Why we gotta wait in line?"

"She does have an in," Naja snapped while looking at me like I was crazy. "We ain't waitin' in line. Let's go." She ushered us toward the front of the club.

"Excuse y'all," one of the bouncers said, lifting the red velvet rope and letting a group of teens in. "The line is back there."

"Okay, but—" I said.

"No buts," he interrupted and pointed. "Now hear what I'm telling you—to the back of line."

"We're here for Haneef," Naja snapped.

"And so is everybody else. Now move along." He pointed toward the end of the line.

"Oh no, he didn't," Mecca said.

Naja turned toward Mecca and Samantha. "It's not as bad as it looks. Bozo is new here and doesn't recognize us from the red carpet." She turned back and looked at the bouncer. "I believe you have it twisted. We're not low-life groupies lying to get inside. We are here to see Haneef, understand? Now stop clownin' and let us through."

The bouncer cracked up laughing, and so did everybody else standing here. "Move!" the bouncer said as he pushed Naja to the side, causing her to stumble. Catching her balance, she looked at him and smiled. "So what does that mean? You not lettin' us in?"

"Excuse me," I said, taking over. Apparently Naja didn't know how to handle this. I batted my eyes at the bouncer.

"Sweetie, can you go get James? He's in Haneef's security."

"Look, y'all wearin' my nerves now. I said stand ya li'l groupie behinds at the end of the line, 'cause in two seconds you're not getting in here period!"

"Groupie?!" Samantha said, taken aback. "Did he call us groupies?"

"I hope y'all didn't bring us all the way over here," Mecca snapped, "to get played."

"Would you shut up?!" I said. I promise you, I wanted to cop this whack ass crew and this bouncer dude in their faces. Punk azzes! I flipped open my cell phone and hoped like heck Haneef picked up his line. After three rings, he answered. "Where you at?" he spat.

Immediately I blushed at him having my number programmed. "Outside, but this line is crazy long. And Debo over here patrolling the door is straight buggin'."

"Debo?" Haneef asked, surprised. "You mean the bouncer?"

"Exactly."

"Ai'ight, hol' up a minute. I'ma send James outside to get you." And he clicked off.

"He said," I looked at the bouncer and smirked, "hol' up a minute."

Naja shot the bouncer a snide grin. "That's what I thought."

"That's more like it," Mecca chimed.

"Uhm hmm," Samantha and Tamara backed her up.

A tall and bald-headed muscular man walked outside the club and looked around. We waved at him and he smiled and walked over to us. "Are you Elite?"

"Yes."

"Alright, come with me, please."

We walked in the club and the place was beautiful. I felt like I had stepped into an ultra-modern showroom. The lower level had black-and-white leather couches placed sporadically around the room. Every corner, crevice, and spot on the floor was like something from *MTV Cribs*. The place was jam-packed from the bottom floor to the rooftop terrace where James led us to.

The place spoke volumes of class, and with each step I felt like I'd arrived. Once we stepped off the glass elevator, I couldn't believe my eyes. Everybody who was anybody was there. It was crazy. Our mouths gaped open as the likes of Rihanna, 50 Cent, Young Buck, Young Berg, Lil Wayne, and on it went jammed past us.

"One second," James said as we stood amazed. "Let me retrieve Haneef."

"Okay . . ." I said in awe, feeling as if I was walking on a cloud. The city lights made the night sky illuminate with hues of red and gold. I understood why the line was so long; it was obvious that this was definitely the place to be.

White-gloved butlers were serving caviar and champagne. One stopped before us. "Would you like—"

And before he could finish, Samantha, Tamara, and Mecca all said, "Sho' would." They lifted the champagne and took the caviar, which was on a wheat cracker bed.

As the waiter walked away, I said, "I can't believe y'all are drinking alcohol. And Naja, you know better."

"Ill?" Mecca frowned. "And what is your deal?"

"You're only seventeen," I said, tight-lipped.

"And what are you, a walking afterschool special?" Samantha gulped down her drink.

"No—"

"Well then, be quiet," Naja said as she sipped.

"Please," Naja said, as she took a drink from another waiter. "Chill. And besides, I'm only gon' have one."

"All I know is that it better be one because I am not down with the drinking and driving."

"You buggin'." She rolled her eyes at me.

"Anyway," Tamara said, "I'm twenty-two. So I can hold my liquor."

"Elite," James said as he walked back over to me. "Come with me, please."

I walked behind him and just as I stopped short to let Evan Ross pass, Naja and the whack crew almost fell on top of me. "Dang, can you back up? And excuse you," I barked at them. "He said Elite."

"Oh no, you didn't just get brand new?" Naja spat.

"What . . . ever," I said, too through with them.

"You're lucky I just spotted 55 Cent staring at me," Naja said.

"It's 50 Cent," Tamara corrected her as they headed in his direction.

"Oh, my God, wait!" Naja screamed at the top of her lungs. "I just spotted R. Kelly! Party on the playground!"

Thankfully, James led me into an area where more celebrities were partying inside a glass room. Haneef was standing beside P-Fifty, one of the hottest hip-hop producers in the business. I took a deep breath and did my best to tame my nervousness, and the butterflies flipping around in my stomach.

Haneef was so fine, it didn't make sense. I pushed my hair behind my shoulders, sucked in my stomach, and walked over to him. I tapped him on the shoulder and he smiled.

"Somebody said," I said as I stood leaning from one leg to the next, while placing my hand on my hip, "that you were looking for this chick."

"I was," he said looking me up and down. "But now that I see you, I'm like forget that chick, what's your name?"

"Li'l Ma," I smiled.

He laughed. "Li'l Ma, ai'ight." He pulled me to his chest for a hug. "Damn, you smell good, girl."

I hoped he couldn't feel my heart racing in my chest.

"Congrats on making platinum," I said as we embraced.

"Thanks. Let me introduce you to P-Fifty."

P-Fifty extended his hand. "Nice to meet you."

Before I could respond, Haneef's publicist cut us off. "Haneef, you're needed on stage." His publicist looked at me. "Hi, and you are?"

"Elite—"

"You remember, she won the radio contest—" Haneef said.

"Oh, great work. Be sure one of the reporters takes a picture, Haneef, and I'll make sure the headline reads how you go the extra mile for your fans."

Fan? What did she just say?

"Anyway," his publicist continued, "it's time for you to give your performance."

Haneef turned toward me and kissed me on the forehead. "Just give me a minute," he said as he walked onto the makeshift stage.

I laid back in the cut, but I could see Naja, Tamara, Samantha, and Mecca blowing kisses, sipping champagne, and waving at celebrities as if they were all good friends. I looked at Naja, and when she took another drink from the butler's tray I walked over to her.

"What are you doing?" I took the drink from her hand.

"What?"

"Why are you drinking?!" I asked in a forceful whisper.

"What, I drank before, girl? Why you buggin?"

"No, you buggin'. You know you're the only one who can drive! And did you forget that you stole your father's car."

"Borrowed."

"Whatever," I pointed at her. "You better get your ass sober before you go home, because if you're too drunk to drive, I'ma be so pissed with you."

"Just watch the performance and stop sweatin' me," Naja said as she walked away.

"Naja," I called behind her but she continued on. I turned back toward the stage, and Haneef winked at me and blew me a kiss. I melted instantly.

Haneef danced and sang the same way he did the first night I saw him in concert. This was fiyah, and the crowd was screaming beyond belief.

After three songs, Haneef walked back and forth across the stage and said, "Ai'ight y'all, before we wrap this up, I wanna sing a special song and I wanna invite Elite"—he looked directly at me—"to sing it with me."

I stood there stunned.

"Elite," Haneef called.

Naja pushed me on the shoulder. "You better go 'head. She's right here!" she pointed.

I tipped out into the crowd and onto the makeshift stage.

At first I was shy, but once I looked into the crowd, I felt the same way I did when Haneef and I first sang together. The feeling in my stomach was crazy and after a few seconds I started to get as psyched as the crowd. Before long, Haneef and I were singing the same duet we'd sung before. This was heaven!

When I was done, everybody was cheering and taking pictures. Imagine that, a crowd filled with celebrities and they were taking pictures of me. For the first time in my life, I felt like my mother had named me the right name . . . Elite.

Haneef grabbed my hand and we took a bow. I stepped offstage and immediately Naja pulled at me, jumping up and down and hugging me. "If you keep this up, we won't have to try out for *American Idol!*"

"*American Idol?*" Immediately that calmed me down because I can't stand Paula. I looked around for Haneef and spotted him talking to Deidra, a Beyoncé type girl with a string of number one hits. A few months back she was rumored to be Haneef's girlfriend. And since he hadn't exactly come out and called me anything other than a fan, I wasn't sure if she was or wasn't.

"Is that Deidra?" Naja asked.

"Yeah."

"Okay, well I'm 'bout to handle this."

"Handle it?" I asked, surprised. "Handle what?"

"I'ma go tell that ho," Naja pointed, "that Haneef is yo' boo—"

"No, don't do that."

"What? Puleeze—" she proceeded to walk toward them.

"No," I snatched her back. "I'm not playing. Don't do that."

For real-for real—this wasn't school; he wasn't Jahaad and she wasn't Ciera. So . . . true story, there was no way I could compete with a chick like Deidra.

Not that she was flyer than me or anything, but still . . . Deidra was a hot superstar and I was a pretty regular around-the-way chick with a buncha drunk friends from the block standing behind me.

"I don't believe this." Naja sucked her teeth.

Deidra was practically standing in Haneef's chest, and she was cheesin' extra hard and long.

"We got a situation?" Tamara said, reeking of alcohol.

"Yeah, and too bad you're too drunk to know what it is," I snapped.

"What's that suppose to mean?"

"Nothing," I said, hating that I felt shy about

walking over to Haneef and interrupting the conversation he was having with Deidra.

"And besides," I spat at Naja as I did my best to fake the funk, "what I care? He ain't my man."

"What?" Naja said, taken aback. "He ain't your man?"

"That's what I said."

"You . . . have lost yo' mind," she said as P-Fifty walked over to us. He nodded at the girls and then smiled at me. "I thought you were real hot tonight. You have a wonderful stage presence." He extended his hand.

"Thank you." I accepted his gesture.

"Yeah," he said while looking me up and down. "Real hot. I hope to see you around again." And he walked away.

Naja and I looked at each other, opened our mouths and silently screamed. It was a wonder my bottom lip wasn't on the floor.

Haneef was still talking to Deidra when I looked his way, and immediately my insecurity came back. He turned around, and then he and Deidra started walking over to me.

Once he was next to me, Haneef held my hand and said, "Deidra, this is Elite and her friends." Then he pointed to each of them as they said their names.

"I'm Naja."

"And I'm Tamara." She elbowed Mecca, who looked as if she were due to throw up at any moment.

"Oh, I'm Mecca."

"And I'm the one and only," she said as she gave a half-drunken smile, "Samantha."

"Nice to meet you."

"Uhmmm hmmm," Naja said. "I bet it is."

Deidra arched her eyebrows and looked at me. "I thought your performance was hot."

"Thank you," I said.

"You're welcome. Ai'ight, Haneef," she smiled a little too hard once again. "I'ma see you around."

"Okay."

Look," Naja tapped me on the shoulder. "I see Lil Wayne over there alone . . . finally. So this is my opportunity to find out why I'm not his number one friend on his MySpace page." She pounded her left fist into the palm of her right hand. "Call me if you need me." She rolled her eyes toward Deidra. "Come on, y'all. I might need backup if Trina come back over here," Naja said to the girls.

As they went on their way, Haneef pulled me by my hand to a secluded corner.

"What are you doing?" I asked him as he hugged me tightly and stroked my hair to the back.

"I missed you."

I looked in his eyes and wondered if he really missed me, or if he was just saying that because it sounded good? "Okay, that's nice."

He stepped back. "So, you didn't miss me?"

"Uhmmmm, maybe."

"Maybe?" And he pulled me to his chest and pressed his lips against mine.

"What, you trying to get a kiss?"

"What," he said as he slipped his tongue into my mouth. "You ain't know?"

And finally, as if we'd been waiting on the cool breeze to blow on a hot summer day, or as if we were the only two in the world and no one else existed, we kissed passionately . . . and true story, I saw stars shooting across the sky and heard birds singing a sweet melody in my ear.

"Excuse me," drifted over our shoulders and broke our kiss. When I looked up, it was Haneef's publicist. "May I speak to you for a moment?" she said.

"Give me a minute," Haneef said to me.

Although I couldn't hear anything, I could tell by the look on his publicist's face that they were talking about me.

A few minutes later they returned, and Haneef led me to the party. I could tell that something was bothering him, but he still showed me a good time. We laughed, danced, and even moved to the level of drinking from the same glass.

I was living the life, except that by the time the night ended, I was even more confused than when I'd started.

When it was time to leave, Naja and the whack crew had overdosed on champagne and being starstruck. I couldn't believe it. They were drunk as skunks, and the only sober one was me . . . but of course, my ass couldn't drive.

I snatched the keys from Naja's hand. "I don't believe this."

"What?" she said as she slid behind the wheel. "I'm sober—ewwwwwww . . ." She stuck her head out the window and started throwing up. The next thing I knew, there was a chain reaction of throwing up going on, and by the time they finished and seemed to be sober again, hours had passed and the early morning sun was sneaking into the sky. Naja looked at me with tears in her eyes and said, "My mother . . . is going to kick . . . my ass."

"And she should, too," I snapped.

"Elite, I have to tell you something."

"What?"

"I still can't drive. I'm too sick."

"Let me get this straight: we sat here all night, you know better than to be drinking anyway, but you did and now a whole day later, you still can't drive. I don't believe this. You're pathetic!"

"I'm sorry, Elite."

"Whatever." I flipped open my phone.

"Who are you calling?" Naja asked in a panic.

"Haneef. I'ma see if he can send someone to pick us up." I dialed Haneef's number at least ten times and each time the call went to voicemail. "Bump it." I looked at Naja. "I'ma call Jahaad." Reluctantly I dialed his number and he answered after the third ring. I could've sworn I heard a female voice when he answered, but I wasn't sure. "What, you got company?" I snapped.

"What, you care?"

"Anyway, can you and one of your boys that can drive come get us."

"Us?"

"Me and Naja, Tamara, Samantha, and Mecca."

"Where are you? And why do I need to bring one of my boys that can drive."

"It's a long story, but Naja can't drive and we have her father's car. So we need someone to drive it back. Can you do it or not?"

"You getting' smart? You're lucky I'm even taking your calls."

"Should I take that as a no?"

He sucked his teeth. "I don't have time to argue with you. Where are you?"

"New York."

"New York!" he screeched.

"Know what? Never mind."

Jahaad sighed. "Where at in New York?"

Reluctantly I gave him the address and an hour later he was pulling up with one of his friends. When he walked over to the car and looked into our faces, he scrunched up his nose. "I see why she couldn't drive."

"Elite," Naja moaned. "I'm sorry."

"Whatever," I said as I headed toward Jahaad's car. I tossed my purse into the backseat.

A few minutes later, Jahaad's friend was driving Naja's dad's car and we were pulling off behind them.

"Why you do me like this, Elite?" Jahaad asked.

I rolled my eyes and sucked my teeth. I knew the feel-sorry-for-me speech was coming. "Do what, Jahaad?"

"Use me. I wanted you so bad last night," he said as he entered the highway.

"Jahaad—" I was cut off by my cell phone ringing. I knew it was either Aniyah or Sydney calling me. It was the first time they'd ever slept in the bed without me, and I knew they were scared. I was hoping Ny'eem stayed with them, and they hadn't been left in the house alone.

I reached in the backseat to grab my purse when I noticed a pair of women's panties on the floor, and beside them was a name bracelet that read Ciera. I couldn't believe it.

"You sleeping with Ciera?!" I snapped.

"What?!"

"You heard me, and here you are trying to make me feel guilty. I don't believe this!" I screamed as he pulled in front of my building.

"What are you talking about?" I took Ciera's name bracelet and threw it in his face. "You figure it out!" I got out of the car and slammed the door.

"Elite!" he called behind me. But I ignored him and kept walking.

SPIN IT . . .

Track 12

I didn't hear from Haneef for two weeks, and it looked to me that I was still stuck with Jahaad. And he was sweatin' me like crazy, begging me to please understand that we were in the same predicament and he was just like me . . . and that he had no idea how the panties and the bracelet had gotten there either.

All I could say to that was: What . . . the . . . hell . . . ever. I was tired of that scenario, Jahaad and Elite no matter the cost. The only problem was I found myself giving in, which was why after a week of Jahaad badgering the hell outta me in school, using up minutes on my phone, I decided to let him convince me to chill with him in New York City at Justin's.

"Elite," Jahaad said as he looked at the menu. "Look, I know we're in New York and all, but check it. True story, with all this money, we could've gone to Crown Chicken on Bergen Street, ordered two kill breasts, a roll, and still had money for the movies. Feel me?"

Was God trying to be funny? Because if he was, I wasn't laughing. This was exactly why I never liked going anywhere with Jahaad—he was the cheapest bastard I knew.

"I gave all my money away to ya mama yesterday," he carried on.

"That was almost a month ago." I rolled my eyes.

"Hmph, whatever. It feels like yesterday."

At that moment, all I could see was me backhanding him across his face.

"I tell you what, though. Since you're suddenly so expensive and everything."

"Expensive?! This was your idea!"

"Well then, since you so receptive to my ideas, understand this: when that waiter comes back, we orderin' one soda"—he held the respective fingers up—"and two straws."

"Why did we even come here, Jahaad? What was the point?"

"To make you feel better about your mother tryna rob you."

My eyes fell from his face. I hated that memory. "This has nothing to do with my mother. This has to do with that heifer's drawers in your car."

"I already told you—"

"A damn lie is what you told me!"

"Excuse me," the waiter said, getting our attention. "Are you ready to order? Would you like to start with something to drink?"

"Yeah," Jahaad said. "We'll have a Sprite and two straws."

I couldn't believe he really ordered that.

"I'll have a glass of water with lemon."

"Lemon?" Jahaad mumbled and looked at me. "That better not be extra." He turned to the waiter. "Bruhman, is that extra?"

"Excuse me?"

"Is there a charge for the lemon?"

"No, sir," the waiter said, looking as if he wanted to laugh.

Once the waiter left the table, I whispered to Jahaad, "You're embarrassing me. If you couldn't afford to bring me here, then you shouldn't have."

"If I didn't have to give your mother a hundred dollars, then maybe we could've been rollin'. I'm not your rich rappin' jump-off."

"I don't have a rich rappin' jump-off! As a matter of fact, do you want your hundred dollars back?" I was sick of him throwing that in my face! I went in my purse and pulled the money out.

"Put that back," he insisted. "You gon' need to pay rent next month, but since I see you're all of a sudden ballin', what you can do is pay half of this bill."

I rolled my eyes. "I ain't paying half of nothing."

"Oh, really? So you got it like that? What, your new boyfriend pays for everything?"

"What are you talking about?! You got a lot of nerve when Ciera's name bracelet and a mysterious pair of dirty behind drawls are in your backseat. And you have the audacity to accuse me of having a rich boyfriend, which by the way, I don't have. Otherwise, I wouldn't be with yo' cheap ass."

"Cheap?" he snapped. "I am not cheap."

"Here you are." The waiter sat the drinks on the table.

"How much is this?" Jahaad asked the waiter.

"Uhmmm, excuse me?"

"The soda," Jahaad pointed. "How much is the soda, my man."

"Oh," the waiter blinked. "Three dollars."

"All that ice and you charging three dollars?" Jahaad sucked his teeth, went in his wallet, pulled out three dollars, and looked at me. "We got fifteen left—order something from the kids' menu. Remember we have to put some gas in the car to get home."

"I'm going to give you two a few minutes," the waiter said. "I'll be back."

He walked away, but before he was even three feet from us, he screamed in laughter.

"Just take me home," I said, embarrassed.

"Oh, now you wanna go home? Let me show you something. Burger King only pays me a few pennies." He went back in his wallet and don't you know, this fool had change spilling from it and falling to the tiled floor. "This is all I got." He pulled a ten, a five, a handful of dimes and nickels, and placed them in the center of the table. I couldn't believe this. "You get the picture now?"

"Good question," came from behind me, and when I looked to see who it was, Haneef was pulling up a chair to the table. He turned the chair around backwards and sat down with his arms hanging over the back. "Oh, my fault." He inched up a little and gave Jahaad a fist bump. "What's good, pot'nah?"

Jahaad was in such shock, he didn't even respond.

"Haneef, what are you doing here?" I said in disbelief.

"I was about to ask you the same thing," he responded.

"Excuse you?" This dude had some nerve! And for real-for real, since I hadn't heard from him, he was lucky I didn't tell him to bounce.

The waiter came over to the table. "Haneef . . ." His eyes were filled with surprise. "Oh, wow! My daughter loves you. You mind giving me an autograph?"

"Not at all, son."

Haneef signed the paper the waiter handed him.

"Thanks a million," the waiter cheesed. He looked at Jahaad and frowned, then turned back to Haneef. "Since you joined the party, would you like to order something?"

"Yeah, hit me with a Sprite."

A Sprite? So he had plans on sitting there long enough to sip on a Sprite?

Okay . . . it was obvious that Haneef played too much. I turned to Jahaad, who was still sitting there in disbelief. There he was getting punked and he was acting like a mannequin. A total turn off. "Uhmmmmm . . ." I folded my lips into my mouth as the waiter quickly returned with Haneef's soda. Haneef took a sip, then looked at me and said, "Let me hollah at you for a minute."

I looked at Jahaad, who had suddenly returned to Earth. "You can't be coming up in here like this." And if I wasn't mistaken, he had poked his chest out.

Finally, this fool was fighting for my honor.

I looked at Haneef as if to say, 'And what you got to say about that?! Teach you not to call me for two weeks.' And for emphasis, I twisted my neck. "Boy, you can't be poppin' up in here thinkin' I'ma just roll out with you."

Haneef stared at me for a moment, and oh, God, I hated that he was fine because it lowered my resistance by the moment. "Whatever," I said.

And wouldn't you know, Haneef laughed. Fell . . . the hell out! "You real funny," he stood up and motioned toward the door. "But for real, I need to hollah at you for a moment."

"Hmmmm, let me think—"

"This is real cute and all, but all this trippin' in public is not gon' wash. Understand? Now I'm asking you nicely, let me speak to you for a moment."

I sucked my teeth and looked at Jahaad. "You better not move!" he said.

I cocked my neck to the side. Okay, tough guy was getting a little out of line with what I better not do. "Just give me a minute."

"Exactly," Haneef said as he nodded his head at Jahaad, placed ten dollars down on the table to cover his drink and tip, and walked out the door.

"You about to bounce with this cat?" Jahaad spat in disbelief.

"No, he probably just wants to talk to me about singing or something. Goodness, I said I'll be right back."

"This is some bullshit!" Jahaad snapped. "I swear, if you walk out that door, when you come back to this table it's gon' be a problem. Won't be no more me and you."

"Dang," I snapped my fingers and then grabbed my purse and excused myself. "Why didn't I leave sooner?"

When I walked out the door and stood in front of the restaurant, Haneef had the audacity to have an attitude. He had some nerve!

"Yo, what are you doing?" he snapped, pacing before me. "I tell you I'm checking for you. I take you on boat rides and invite you to V.I.P. to chill with me, and you out with some dude?"

"Excuse you, last I checked you weren't my man. I was a fan, remember? One you were anxious to please."

"Well—"

"Well hell, I'm tired of playing with you. One minute we cool, I think that maybe you feeling me, and then you say some stupid shit like you expect me to remain a groupie. Well, to hell with that."

"So what you sayin'? That's your man?"

"I'm sayin' that you're not. And you know what? Yeah, yeah, that's my man."

Haneef took a step back. "Dead that shit."

Now I took a step back. "Dead what?"

"Ole boy."

"You might wanna ask me if I want to be with him."

"Do you?"

"No."

"Ai'ight then, I said dead it."

"You don't tell me what to do! You're not my man."

"Ai'ight, how about this? I like you. I more than like you. I'm straight diggin' you, and I want you to come and chill with me. Now I'll admit that maybe I've been seeming a little indecisive—"

"A little—?"

"But I'm not anymore, and I wanna chill with you. That's if you wanna chill with me."

I stood there for a moment. I couldn't believe all that was happening. On the one hand, I had the bozo I'd been with for four years taking me for granted, and on the other hand, I had my dream date telling me how he felt about me. It felt like a dream.

"Yeah," I nodded. "I think we can chill."

He pointed to his Hummer, where his driver was holding open the back door. "After you."

I slid in and as we blended into traffic, I saw Jahaad coming out of Justin's looking for me.

SPIN IT . . .

Track 13

I didn't know if I was I on the run, or if I had just been kidnapped. I knew for sure that Jahaad and I were a wrap and there was no turning back. But I wondered about everything else in my life. For a moment I felt like everything was going by so fast, and I wasn't sure if time was passing by exactly the way I wanted it to.

"What you thinking about, Li'l Ma?"

"Honestly, I'm thinking about how my life is zooming by and I'm not so sure if I want it to go that fast. You know what I mean?"

"Well, I guess it depends on what's happening in your life that would make you feel like that."

"Just . . ." I hesitated. "Some things."

"Do you think you're not living your dream, and may never get to?"

I shifted in my seat and stared at him. I thought

about how he'd gone from the poster on my ceiling, to the voice on my radio, to the person in the flesh who was sitting next to me. "I think I'm pretty close." I scooted closer to him.

He flicked my nose. "I like you, Li'l Ma. I really do."

"Why, though?"

"Because you're real," he said instantly. "And I know you're not doing this for publicity or anything other than really diggin' me, and I like that. And I know I'm here and I'm there, never really in one place for long, but right now I just want you to flow with me and somehow," he said as we pulled up in front of a roller skating rink, "we gon' do this."

"Is that so?"

"That's more than so." He smiled and kissed me on the lips. "Now, are you ready for this?" he nodded at the entrance.

"Boy, you better stop playing with me. You know I'm from the hood, right?"

"The hood?"

"Exactly, so you must've brought me here so I can teach you how to skate."

"You wish," he said as his driver opened the door.

"I see I'ma have to teach you a lesson," I laughed, walking toward the door. But before I knew anything, I was up in the air. "Put me down!" I laughed so hard I cried as Haneef tossed me over his shoulder. "Stop."

"Nah." He started to tickle me. "You talkin' too slick."

I hadn't laughed that hard in a long time. Tears flooded my eyes and I was blinded by the time we walked inside. Haneef handed me a tissue and as I wiped my face, I noticed that besides his driver and security, we were the only ones in the place.

"Where are all the people?" I asked as he started to put on his skates.

"Home, I guess. What size skate you wear?"

"Seven, but . . . I've never been to a roller rink where there were no people."

"That's because," he said as he handed me a new pair of skates, "you've never been anywhere where I rented out the place."

"Dang, it's like that?" I sat down and started putting on my skates.

"What, you ain't know?" Haneef said as he started to skate and dance to Frankie Beverly and Maze's, "Before I Let Go." That song was a serious throwback and it reminded me of my mother. She loved herself some oldies and on a good day, she loved to skate!

Haneef and I skated and danced the whole night through. We laughed, kissed, hugged, ate, and plain and simply bugged out. I'd never had this much fun on a date in my life. It almost made being subjected to Jahaad's cheap antics worth it.

By the time the night ended and we were parked in front of Naja's house, I knew for sure I could do this for a while.

"I had a good time, Li'l Ma."

"Me, too," I said as he kissed me.

"So I'ma see you soon, right?"

"Yeah," I said as his driver opened the door for me. "Real soon, I hope."

I stood in front of Naja's house as Haneef pulled away, and just as he turned the corner, I saw my mother and Gary sitting on the steps of an abandoned building up the block, and I was back to drowning in my reality.

SPIN IT . . .

Track 14

"Wake up, sleepyhead."

I couldn't remember the phone ringing. All I knew was that I answered it. "Haneef?" I peeled one eye open.

"The one and only."

I looked at the clock, which read six a.m. "Do you know what time it is?"

"Time to get up."

I stretched. It was obvious he'd gone crazy, from stalking me to this.

"Come chill with me this morning," he said.

"Chill with you? You just kidnapped me two days ago."

"Funny. Come on and wake up."

"Alright," I yawned.

"Ill, you don't have to come. All yawning in my ear."

"My fault."

"Ai'ight, now get up, sleepyhead. Unless you know you don't wanna come, and then I'm sure I can get at least a thousand chicks to come and chill with me. After all, I am Haneef—"

"Are you on yourself, or what?"

"I'm just sayin'."

"Haneef."

"What?"

"Be quiet and come get me."

An hour later I was dressed and shaking Ny'eem on his shoulder. "Wake up." I tapped the heel of my stiletto.

"Man," he stirred, "if you don't get out of here . . ." He pulled the cover over his head.

"Wake up!" I shook him again, only harder this time.

"What?" He turned over and looked at me like I was crazy.

"I'll pay you ten dollars if you stay home this morning and see about the kids."

"Do what?"

"See about the kids."

"Me stay home and with kids?" he laughed. "Yeah, imagine that . . ."

"Alright, twenty dollars."

"Nope—not me. Ya boy don't do kids like that." He turned back over to sleep.

"Fifty dollars."

"Fifty?" He turned back toward me. "How long you gon' be gone?"

"Two hours." I crossed my fingers behind my back.

"Two hours?" he said suspiciously. "And you gon' pay me fifty dollars?"

"Yeah."

"Ai'ight . . . I'll do it."

"Straight." I grabbed my purse and keys, and handed him five dollars.

"What the hell—"

"I'ma need to go on a payment plan." And I ran out the door before he could stop me.

By the time I walked down the street to Naja's, Haneef was pulling up. His driver got out and opened the door.

"Why are you always walking from down the street instead of coming out the front door of your house?"

"Uhm . . . my grandmother . . . lives down the street and I always check on her in the morning. So anyway," I wanted desperately to change the subject, "where are we going?"

"My place."

"Yo' place?" I said, taken aback. "I know you don't think you about to get no booty?"

"Oh, I can't get none?" He started tickling me. "What—what—so what's really good with you?"

"Okay, stop now." I laughed until I cried.

"Look," Haneef said, sweeping my hair to the

back, away from my face. "Chill, if you good, then I'm good. I like you and while I'm home for a while, I wanna kick it wit' you. You ai'ight with that?"

"Yeah," I smiled at him. "I'm fine with that."

"Cook? Who you think 'spose to cook? I thought you were rich?"

"I am," Haneef laughed.

"Then what are you tryna get a bootleg meal outta me for? Boy, please stop playing with me and call up a chef."

Haneef laughed so hard he was bending over at the waist. We were at his New York City apartment. He lived in a high-rise building with mad security in the lobby. I saw at least a dozen celebrities and even more socialites in the lobby as we headed up to his place.

Haneef lived on the top floor and his view was amazing. His apartment looked exactly the way it did when he was on *MTV Cribs:* endless walls of windows, black leather furniture, plasma screen TVs, a movie room, *Star Trek* posters, his collection of miniature cars, every movie and video game you could imagine, and platinum singles hung like artwork.

He had a gourmet kitchen which was real fly and opened to the living room area. I hopped on the barstool at his marble top kitchen island and looked around. True story, one corner of this place was bigger than the subsidized apartment I lived in.

I twisted my lips and glared at this dude as if he'd lost a few screws. I may have played mother to my brothers and sisters, but cooking was something I didn't do.

"How about this?" Haneef said when he'd stopped laughing so hard. "Since you too fly to cook, I'ma stir up some grub for you."

"Stir up some grub? Does that sound appetizing to you? Nah, I'm good. I can pass."

"I got skills, girl."

"Uhmmm hmmm," I twisted my lips again. "I'm sure you do."

"Watch ya boy at work and learn something."

Haneef opened his refrigerator and took out crab meat, shrimp, and scallops, a pack of linguini noodles, and broccoli. He sautéed the crab meat, shrimp, and scallops in a butter sauce, boiled the noodles, and steamed the broccoli. About an hour later, he had made a full gourmet meal.

"Dang, boo," I said in awe as I watched him set the table. "My fault for doubting you."

"You know how I do it." He smiled. "Now come on and let's eat." He pulled me in a chair with him, took his fork, and began to feed me. I was in Heaven. "This is so good."

"Oh, now it's good?" he teased.

"Yes," I said, kissing him and mushing a linguini noodle between our lips.

"So . . ." Haneef asked after we were done eating. "You still doubting me?"

"Yeah," I said seriously.

"What? What are you still doubting?"

"If you're too good to be true."

Haneef cupped my chin and kissed me. "I'm real, baby. Every part of me is real." He stared in my eyes and when I felt tears sneaking into my throat, I knew I had to change the subject. So I stood up and grabbed his Wii control.

"You know how to box?"

"Box?" he said, taken aback. "You wanna kick it about a game?"

"Yeah." There was no way I was gonna take the chance of becoming too emotional so that the next thing I knew, I was confessing a buncha shit I didn't want anyone to know about me. "What, you scared?" was my attempt to punk him.

"Nah, are you?" he asked me.

I didn't respond to that question. Instead I said, "You must be scared of me whuppin' yo' butt."

"Oh what, you ain't heard?"

"Heard what?"

"King Kong ain't got nothin' on me."

"You are so corny." I laughed. "Now come on so I can give you a Nintendo Wii boxing beat-down."

"Ai'ight." He took the other control. "Let's roll."

We started boxing and I started throwing a left hook, ducking his right, but not seeing the upper cut. I fell to the floor. Ai'ight, ai'ight, I can get it together. I took it to his chest, slammed him with a right hook, and then a left one. Snuck him with a upper cut, and the next thing I knew he was down!

I started jumping up and down. "I'm queen of the world!"

In fact, I was jumping up and down so much, I didn't even notice how he'd somehow gotten up and beat me down. The screen said game over and his figure was the one holding the belt.

"You cheated!" I screamed. "I wanna rematch!"

He laughed. "Yeah, ai'ight. You were so busy yelling that you were queen of the world, that you got caught slippin'."

"Whatever." I placed the remote down and flopped down on the sofa. "To heck with that stupid game."

"Ah, my Li'l Ma mad." He sat beside me and placed his head in my lap. "I like you, Li'l Ma. You know that?"

"I like you, too."

"How much?"

"This much." I bent down and kissed him on his lips.

By the time I got home, the kids were in the bed and Ny'eem was on the couch asleep. When I tried to sneak past him, he opened one eye. "That was real foul what you did."

"Ny'eem," I whined. "I didn't expect to be gone that long."

"Yeah, right. So where did you go?"

"You really wanna know?" I smiled.

"Yeah."

"Ai'ight. I went on a date with Haneef!"

"Haneef, like that singin' dude?"

"Yeah." I flopped down on the couch next to him. "It was like the best date I ever had in my life."

"So wassup with Jahaad?"

"Ja-who? You mean Ja-loser. I told him to get lost."

Ny'eem cracked up. "That's wassup. I couldn't stand him anyway."

"Ny'eem, it was the best date ever."

"Who went on a date?" My mother flew through the front door, and for the first time in a long while she came in with a bag of groceries.

"You went to the grocery store, or you got a five finger discount?" Ny'eem asked.

"You being smart?"

"Well Ma, I was thinking the same thing. It is like almost one o'clock in the morning."

"Don't worry about what time it is, just know there's some food for y'all. So who went on a date?"

"Elite," Ny'eem spat quickly.

"With who?" My mother started putting the food up.

"Haneef," I said.

"The rappin' reggae dude?"

"He sings hip-hop, Ma."

"Same thing." My mother opened a carton of chocolate ice cream, sat three bowls on the table, and filled them.

I rolled my eyes to the ceiling as I took my

bowl and spoon. "It's not. Anyway . . . I had the best time of my life."

"What y'all do?" Ny'eem asked, taking his bowl and eating his ice cream.

I told my mother and Ny'eem everything that Haneef and I did. From the food he cooked, to the boxing match, everything.

The only part I left out was how embarrassed I was about was our life.

"Can you image, Lee-Lee," my mother said, finishing her bowl of ice cream, "if you were famous?"

"What would you do, Ma?"

"I would get clean."

Ny'eem and I sat quiet, both of us looking as if we'd just been reminded that we were a crackhead's kids. "I'ma get ready to go to bed, Ma," I said, placing my bowl in the sink.

"Yeah," Ny'eem said. "Me, too."

And we both left our mother in the kitchen watching us retreat to the other room. The last thing I wanted to fantasize about was something that wasn't going to come true.

SPIN IT . . .

Track 15

"Elite and Naja," Thelma said to us as she looked over the store's ledger, "I'm going to start to do the inventory."

Instantly my heart dropped and I looked at Naja. I had so much stuff to return it was crazy.

"Why?" I hoped she couldn't sense the nervousness in my voice.

"Because some of our things have gone missing."

"Missing?" Naja asked, surprised. "What?"

"Yeah, I'm hoping that it's misplaced or something." I gave Naja an "I told you so look," and then I said to Thelma, "Okay, if you want to do inventory, then no problem," I smiled. "Less work for me."

Thelma smiled back and then she walked into

back of the store. "We gon' have to return that stuff," I said to Naja.

"I know."

I shook my head. "I hate I ever started doing that shit."

"Me, too."

"Are you closing this week?" Naja asked.

"No, but I hope to be soon."

SPIN IT . . .

Track 16

It was spring break and school was closed all week because the teachers were having an in-service day. Which all added up to this: I could chill with Haneef extra hard!

And although I really couldn't afford it, I was still making payment arrangements with Ny'eem to pay him fifty dollars to see about the twins and Mica each time I hung with Haneef. I think my bill was reaching toward five hundred dollars. Whatever. Anyway, even though he kept the kids during the day, I came home at night. I didn't get it twisted.

However, early each day, I was always up, standing in front of Naja's house, and Haneef was always there to scoop me. We spent time at his apartment in the city, rode his boat, walked (with crazy security) through Central Park, and just straight chilled.

Often times I forgot he was a celebrity, until a screaming fan would come from nowhere and start crying his name, and then I would be like oh, yeah . . . I was walking with *the* Haneef.

We planned a real fly trip one day. Haneef chartered a small plane to fly us to Miami. I was thinking of palm trees, beach, and shopping! Scratched that, though. I wanted to say damnyummm . . . !

The only problem was I couldn't find Ny'eem that morning. I needed this li'l dude to bring his ass home. I'd deal with him later about where he'd gone and when he'd snuck out.

"What you gon' do?" Naja asked as I stood watching out the window and holding the telephone to my ear.

I hated stupid questions. If I knew what I was going to do, I would have been doing it. Right? "Naja," I sighed, "don't ask me questions I can't answer."

"I could always go in your place."

"Don't play with me."

She laughed. "Well you have to think of something."

"I know . . . oh, and don't be telling my business to ya new homegirls, Samantha and Mecca, either."

"What? Why you say that?"

"Because I don't like them being all in my business."

"You think they're all in your business? I just thought they were in everybody else's business."

"Naja, please." My other line beeped. I looked at the caller ID and it was Ny'eem. "Hold on, this is Ny'eem." I clicked over. "Where are you?!"

"I'm out making some moves."

"Excuse me?" I said, taken aback. "Making moves doing what?"

"Minding my business," he snapped. "Now look, I'ma be home later tonight."

"Tonight! I need you home now. I need you to see about the kids."

"Lately, I'm always with them kids. I swear, you and that li'l rap dude are taking advantage of me. Come on, give me a break!"

"I wanna go out for once and now you're complaining about you're always with them! Ny'eem, I oughta punch you in the face!"

"Man, please."

"I'm always with those kids!" I screamed.

"Well, then it shouldn't be that hard for you to be with them today, because I'm not gon' be home." And he clicked off.

I clicked back over and screamed at the top of my lungs! I could hear Naja scrambling with the phone. "What the hell was that?!" she spat. "I think you just broke my eardrum."

"He said he's not coming home!"

"What?" she said. "He's moving out?"

"No, I mean today."

"He's moving out for a day? Huh? I'm confused."

I blew out a slow string of air. "Ahhhh!!!!!" I screamed again. "Dang, Naja, he can't babysit."

"Well damn, you can calm down. That's all you had to say in the first place. All that other stuff was extra."

"Anyway . . ."

"Yeah, anyway, what you gon' do?"

"Uhmmmm . . ." I shook my head. "Can you . . . ?"

"Can I what?"

"Maybe, like baby—"

"Oh no, I'm sorry. I don't do kids."

Before I could respond, my other line beeped. I looked at the caller ID and it was Haneef. "Hold on," I sighed. "Hello."

"Dang, Li'l Ma," Haneef said. "Why you sound like somebody just robbed you?"

"Because they did."

"Huh?" he said, put off.

"Look, Haneef . . . I can't go. My brother just said he can't keep the kids—"

"What kids? I thought you said you didn't have any children."

"Children? I don't have any children. I mean my sisters and brother."

"Where's your mother?"

"Uhm . . . working . . . yeah . . . at the . . . at the . . . bus station."

"Bus station?" I could hear the confusion in his voice. "I thought she was a nurse?"

Damn, I forgot that lie. "Yeah, that's what I mean. And my dad—"

"Isn't he dead?"

Dang, how the heck did I forget that, too? This lying was a hot mess. "Look, the bottom line is I can't go because there's no one here to keep my sisters and brother, and I can't leave them home alone."

"Bring them with you."

"Excuse me?" I wasn't sure I'd heard him right. "Say that again."

"Bring them with you. It'll be fun. Instead of flying to Miami, I'll tell the pilot that we'll go to Disney World."

"Are you serious?"

"Elite," he said, sounding sweet as ever, "it's cool. Bring them."

"Oh . . . uhmmm . . ."

"I'm not taking no for an answer."

"Haneef . . ."

"I'm serious. Just get them dressed."

"Are you sure?"

"What did I just say?"

"Alright. How long before you come?"

"An hour—so hurry up."

I wasn't sure if I said bye when I clicked off or not. And I was sure Naja had hung up, so I didn't even bother to call her back. Instead, I ran into the bedroom and screamed, "Get up!" The twins stirred and I pulled the covers off them. "Get up! We have somewhere to go."

"Where?!"

"Disney World!"

They jumped out of bed and started screaming.

I ran in my mother's room that she never occupied and woke up Mica.

"Mica!"

He jumped up and the sheet he loved to hang on to wrapped around his body like a tape.

"Help me," he mumbled.

I untangled him. "We're getting' ready to go."

"Go where?"

"Disney World."

"Hot damn!"

I balled up my fist. "What I tell you about cussin'?!"

"I'm sorry."

"You better be. Now get up. We're going out."

Forty-five minutes later the kids were in short sets and sweaters. I had on a pair of cargo capris and a matching tee.

By the time we walked to the entrance of the building, every crackhead who lined the hall looked at us like we'd lost our minds. "It's cold outside," my mother said as she seemed to emerge from nowhere.

"I know," I snapped, trying my best to move past her.

"We're going to Disney World," Mica said.

Gary, who was standing beside my mother, fell out laughing. "You sure they ain't gettin' high?" And as usual, it was on.

"What I tell you about my kids?" my mother screamed. And we left them standing there.

It was cold outside and maybe we should've put on some jeans, but so what? We were going to Disney World, some place we'd only seen in magazines.

"Looka hear, my man." Mica said, shivering cold, as Haneef's driver opened the back door to his Hummer. "Next time, come get us from the house. We shouldn't have to walk all the way down here. It's cold out here. Smell me?"

"Shut up!" I said tight-lipped, and mushed him slightly in the back of his head.

"You must be Mica," Haneef smiled as Mica slid in the truck.

"Haneef!" Sydney jumped up and down. "Oh, my God!!!!! Wait 'til I call the girls in my class: Kennesha, Donnesha, Tamika, Theresa, Jona, Octavia—"

"See," Aniyah did her best to whisper. "I told you she wasn't lying."

"Funny," I grimaced. "And I told you all that you better behave, and don't talk too much—"

"Chill," Haneef laughed, seemingly getting a kick out of them. "They're alright."

"Yeah," Sydney snapped. "Didn't we leave Mommy in the hallway?"

Oh . . . kay. I saw I was gonna have to handle this crew. Maybe bringing them with me was a bad idea. "Be quiet," I pointed. "Now look out the window."

“Ill,” Sydney whispered loudly. “She actin’ real stank.”

I looked at them and shot them such a serious evil eye, it’s a wonder I didn’t burn a hole through their chests.

“Okay,” Sydney said, waving her hands in defeat. “We get it, we get it.”

“Fa’ real,” Aniyah added. “No need in being all extra.”

Once we were all in the car and on our way to the airport, Haneef asked, “So have you guys ever been on a plane before?” He slyly pulled me next to him by my belt loop and draped his arm over my shoulder. Oh . . . he felt so good.

After talking about how this was going to be our first plane ride, we laughed at some of Haneef’s corny jokes, Sydney did what she could to secure herself a record deal, and I had to threaten Aniyah when she wanted to tell Haneef how much of a fan of his I really was.

Before we knew it, we were at a small airport in New York, ready to board the small chartered plane.

“Elite,” Mica whispered as he pulled the hem of my shirt. “I wanna ask you something.”

“What?”

“Sydney said that when it rains, that’s people peein’ outta airplanes. So you think we’ll have time to change the weather from a bright sunny day to a stormy one?”

I did all could to not fall out laughing. "Mica, don't believe that."

"It's not true?!" he said in disbelief.

"No."

Tears filled his eyes. "So I drank all this water for nothing?" he said, exhausted. "I'm so tired of being lied to."

When we boarded the plane, it resembled something out of a magazine, or better yet, something off *MTV Cribs*, just in the air and not on the ground.

There were about ten beige oversized leather recliners, and a glass bar stacked with juices, cakes, bagels, and donuts. There were two sixty-inch flat-screen TVs, a PlayStation, a Wii, at least a thousand games, and two DVD players with tons of movies. And the bathroom was bigger than the one we had at home. It even had a jacuzzi in it! A jacuzzi! On a plane! It was crazy.

"Dang!" Aniyah said in complete awe. "This cat must be pay'yaid!"

"Fa'sho," Sydney said as she flopped back in the leather recliner and put her feet up. "You done good fa ya'self, Elite." She animated her voice like an old country lady.

We all laughed and Haneef whispered, "Yeah Elite, you done real good." He walked up behind me and kissed the back of my neck. Then he slid his left arm over my respective shoulder and slid his right hand in my side pocket, "You all wanna go and meet the pilot?" he asked my sisters and brother.

Their eyes popped open wide. "Yeah!"

"Ai'ight," he said. "See that door?" he pointed. "His name is Pilot Mitchell and he's a real cool dude. We have a few minutes before takeoff, so he'll be happy to show you around."

"Yay!" they cried as they skipped off. Once they were behind the pilot's door, I felt more like a mother watching her children than an older sister, especially knowing that the trip was something none of us would ever forget.

Once they disappeared from sight, Haneef turned toward me and held me by my waist. I slid my arms around his neck.

"You know, Mica reminds me of myself when I was his age," he said.

"What? You walk around with a sheet, too?" I laughed.

"A sheet? What sheet?"

"Nothing, forget it. Finish telling me what you were saying."

He kissed me lightly on the lips. "He reminds me of when I was a little boy and my brothers used to look out for me."

"Really?" I kissed him back.

"Yeah, I used to go everywhere with my brothers, even when I didn't want to." He kissed me again.

"Why?" I asked as our lip teasing turned into a passionate embrace.

"Ai'ight, ai'ight," I said, breaking our lip lock and wiping my gloss from his mouth. "We need to stop."

"Why?" he tried to kiss me again.

"Because we have kids behind that door."

"So?"

"Haneef, I cannot have them see me kissing you."

"You act too old for your age. You know that, right?"

"Whatever." I sat down in one of the recliners and crossed my legs. "So tell me, why were you always with your brothers?"

"Because my mother was always working." He sat down on my lap but I pushed him in his back. "Get your big butt off me!" I cracked up laughing and he began tickling me. "Oh, I can't sit on you?" He tickled my stomach. "Oh, what—say it—"

I was laughing so hard, tears were pouring from my eyes. "Would you get up?"

"I'm buggin', Li'l Ma," he said, sitting in the recliner beside me, and pulling me onto his lap.

"Haneef."

"Wassup?"

"How did you get your start in music?"

"Remember how I said my mother was always working?"

"Yeah."

"Well, that's how I met P-Fifty and got into music. He and my oldest brother went to school together. We went to his house one day, and it was on from there."

"Wow," I smiled. "I betchu your mother doesn't work that much now," I laughed.

"Yeah, something like that. Now, tell me again what your mother does."

"She's . . . a waitress . . . I mean, a bus—nurse."

"A who?"

"A nurse."

Haneef shook his head and kissed me again. "Ai'ight." He shrugged his shoulders.

"You know you can tell me anything," he said.

"Okay." I nodded my head.

"And you know," he continued, "I've been thinking about how we've been chillin'."

"Really?"

"Yeah and true story, everywhere I go, I'm always thinking about you."

"You're making me blush." I laid my head against his chest.

"I'm dead serious."

He stood up and pulled me closer on his lap.

"Do you think about me?" he asked.

"All the time," I said without hesitation. "And when I'm not around you, I miss you like crazy."

"Me, too, Li'l Ma. I wanna show you the world."

"You wanna show me the world?" I lifted my head from his chest and looked into his face in disbelief.

"Man, Elite, nothing is too good for you."

I swallowed and didn't know why, but tears rushed to my eyes and I felt like I was gonna break down and cry. It was stupid, and I needed to be stronger than that. "Yeah?" I said so low I don't know whether he heard me or not.

"I mean," he went on, "you're real special. And I was thinking that I needed to ask you to be my girl."

Holding back the tears were a done deal; they were rolling freely down my cheeks. "What?" He wiped them away. "You don't wanna be my girl?"

I shook my head up and down.

"Then tell me." He cupped my chin.

"I just never had anyone . . ." I couldn't even speak I was crying so hard. "I just . . ."

"Just what, Li'l Ma?"

"I don't know . . ." I wiped my eyes. I felt so dumb.

"You don't know if you wanna be with me?"

I looked at him as if he was crazy. "Of course I wanna be with you. Yes. Yes. I'll be your girl. I am your girl. Yes."

He smiled. "Good, and you know, it's no secrets between us. I'll never lie to you, and you don't have to lie to me."

I nodded my head, though I realized much of what he knew about me was a lie.

He took his platinum chain with the diamond microphone that hung around his neck and placed it on me. "This way, everybody'll know that you're my girl."

Tears filled my eyes again, but this time they were tears of joy. I drew my face into his and we kissed like no tomorrow. It was official; it was the best day of my life.

"Ooooole . . ." Mica, Sydney, and Aniyah said as if they were a soprano chorus.

"I'm tellin' . . ." Aniyah sang. "Mediatakeout. com. . . ."

The first face we saw when we arrived in Disney World was Mickey Mouse's and of course the ghetto hoods, better known as Mica, Aniyah, and Sydney, bum-rushed him.

"Mickey," Mica said, "how come I don't see you around my way?"

"Cause he ain't tryna get jacked," Sydney snapped. "A name like Mickey Mouse, he'd be played out."

"Fa' real," Aniyah nodded her head. "And with all that red and black he got on," she said as she looked him up and down, "best believe whenever he step foot in Brick City, it's gon' be a situation."

Oh . . . my . . . God . . . I was embarrassed. "Stop actin' like y'all ain't never been nowhere."

"Block parties don't count." Sydney rolled her eyes at me as they proceeded toward a group of water rides.

"Hey y'all!" Haneef said. "Wanna race?!"

"Haneef—"

"Man, loosen up." He smiled at me and then back at Mica. "You game?"

"Haneef, maybe some people think you can

sing," Mica said with confidence, "but I really don't think you tryna get humiliated out here."

We all fell out laughing. "Oh, so what you sayin'? You got some skills?"

"I'm not one to brag," Mica said as he popped his collar, "but since you asked."

"Ai'ight, so let go!"

"Haneef, you really don't have to," I said tight-lipped as I watched his security team shake their heads. "Look sweetie, Mica's a sore loser, and I really don't feel like hearing him cry."

Haneef ignored me. "Come on, man." He and Mica squatted in racing positions, "On your mark . . . get set . . . go . . . !" And Mica took off so fast, Haneef didn't even see him leave the start line.

"How in the heck—?" Haneef half shielded his eyes.

"Tried to warn you. You cannot outrun a kid from the hood."

He hooked me playfully around my neck. "Whatever!" and we laughed all the way through the series of water rides we took for the next hour. Afterwards, we played all sorts of games, won prizes, rode every roller-coaster you could image, and when it was all over and time to go, we were exhausted.

By the time we boarded the plane, we all fell asleep and didn't wake up until we were back in New York, where we got in Haneef's Hummer, and he brought us home.

“Thanks for everything,” I said to Haneef as we pulled up in front of Naja’s.

“Anytime. I had fun.” He kissed me.

“Me, too.” I kissed him back. “Well,” I said sadly, “I need to get in the house.”

“Alright, call me.” He hopped in his Hummer and as he turned the corner, we walked home, stepped over the crackheads, went in the apartment, where I cried myself to sleep.

SPIN IT . . .

Track 17

"So you and Jahaad not together no more?" Samantha caught me and Naja as we grabbed our food and headed toward the lunch table.

"Why?" We sat down and before long, Mecca was on our heels. Samantha passed us as we sat our food down, and she rolled her eyes so hard at me I thought she was going to trip over 'em. Whatever.

"Who she looking at crazy?" Naja snapped.

"I don't know," I retorted. "But as long as she keeps my name out of her mouth, then we straight. Otherwise—"

"It's gon' be a situation."

"Exactly." I turned back to Samantha. "Now, what you say?"

"She said," Mecca butted in, "are you and Jahaad over with?"

"How y'all know?"

"The whole school knows, "Samantha replied.

"Ciera walking around here blasting it!" Mecca exclaimed. "She was all loud in homeroom, making a major announcement about it like somebody really cared."

"What she say?" Naja asked.

I sucked my teeth. I couldn't believe this.

"She said—" a smirk ran across Samantha's face—"that they been bone'n and on the creep since sometime early last year."

"Uhmmm," Mecca said. "That's what she said. You know they wrong. But I heard that Ciera had been pregnant . . . twice, had a miscarriage, and the whole nine."

"I heard that, too," Samantha said in awe, as if she were surprised they'd heard the same things.

I was pissed, especially because ever since we picked up this clique and they somehow inducted themselves into our crew, they'd been in my business. "You think I care? Please," I laughed it off, "what . . . the . . . hell . . . ever!"

"Oh," Naja said, taken aback. "But me, I'm pissed off!"

"Well then," Mecca went on, "get ready for this, since you don't care."

"I know what you about to say," Samantha chimed in.

"What?" Mecca asked.

"That Ciera said Jahaad told her that Elite's mother was a crackhead."

I almost fell on the floor.

"What?!" Naja screeched.

"And I heard," Mecca said, "that he had to pay their rent for the last year. That he was giving your mother money, and that you, Elite, were just using him and that's why you hooked up with Haneef, because you are usin' him, too!"

I didn't know if anyone saw me, but I passed the hell out. I felt like barging in Jahaad's classroom, or squattin' on him in the cafeteria and kicking his ass. I swallowed and prayed like hell that I played this off. "Like I said before, what . . . the . . . hell . . . ever. Please, if anything, his grandmother's on crack and she sell her ass!"

"Boom!" Naja snapped. "There it is!"

"Now run and take that back."

Mecca and Samantha fell out laughing.

And I did, too. Cept the thing behind the upward curl of my lips and the sound coming out of my mouth was my chest burning and my heart skipping a thousand beats at the threat of being exposed. And yeah, there were a thousand girls like me with mothers on drugs and all of that—but that was not what I really wanted people to see. Regardless of the rest of the world, I was very protective of my family.

As the girls continued to laugh and chat amongst themselves, only Naja noticed I'd stopped smiling. Samantha and Mecca were carrying on and gossiping about everybody who came our way.

When the bell rang and we gathered our trays

and headed back to class, Naja pulled me to the side.

"You think Jahaad really did that?"

"How else would they know?"

"Well, we just have to spread some rumors about him and Ciera."

"Yeah . . ." I said reluctantly, knowing that would only lead to more trouble. "We just might."

SPIN IT . . .

Track 18

Haneef and I had been kickin' it strong for the last month, and I felt like maybe . . . I could really be happy. The only thing was, Haneef still didn't know the real deal about my life. He thought I lived a ghettohood fairy tale, when all the while it was a nightmare.

Long gone were the days of paying Ny'eem to stay home; I couldn't find him long enough to even make him the offer. So, I started going out in the early evening or right after work, so it didn't look so bad to the twins and Mica that I wasn't home as much as I used to be.

Ny'eem had been staying out later and later. His teachers were calling the house nonstop and my mother was too high to see what it was all about. But I'd reached the point where I had to let go of my worries about losing Ny'eem to the streets, and deal with the kids I still had to care for. But somehow in the quiet of night, I worried about how I was gonna get Ny'eem to see what was right.

I turned over to sleep and moved Sydney's feet out of my face when I heard a loud banging on the front door, followed by my bedroom door flying open. "Elite!" I jumped up. It was my mother, crying and in a panic.

"What? What's wrong?!"

"They just locked up Ny'eem. Put your clothes on. We got to go."

"They what? Who is they?"

"The police just locked him up. We need to go get him!"

"Where'd they arrest him?"

"In front of the building," she said as she wiped tears from her eyes. "When I told them he was my son and asked what the problem was, they said he was selling drugs."

"Selling what?" I couldn't believe this, but then again, I could. "When did this happen?"

"Just a second ago. Now put on your clothes. We got to go and get my boy!"

"Ma, calm down."

Tears were flying from her eyes and she was shaking. "I can't do it," she shook her head. "I can't have y'all be like me."

"Then you need to be a better you!" I snapped.

"Excuse me?"

"You heard me. Dang, Ma. Ny'eem is in jail and

you're coming to get me like I'm the mother. You have to go down there. Even if they release him, he can only be released into an adult's custody."

"Say you eighteen."

"Ma! They ask for ID. Why can't you go down there?"

"Because I'm scared," she cried. "I'm scared."

I stood silent. I didn't know what to do, what to say, or how to feel. Here was my mother crying like she was the child, and I was the adult. The only problem was there was no way we could reverse roles, at least not in this situation.

"Ma, just try. Try to go down there and see what happens."

"I don't want anything to happen to my boy."

"Ma, go and see."

She wiped her eyes, arched her back, and left the room.

I paced the living room for three hours, hoping and praying that things turned around. And just as a steel lump filled my throat, a key jingled in the lock and the knob twisted. It was my mother. "Where is Ny'eem?"

"In jail."

My heart stopped. "What? Why? Why didn't they let him go?"

"They said he had too many charges."

"Charges?"

"Something about a stolen car . . ." She broke down again. "I can't believe this. This is all my fault. All my fault."

"You're right," I said coldly. "It is."

SPIN IT . . .

Track 19

"Elite," Naja whispered as we sat in the back of the bus on our way to school. "I heard that Ciera is pregnant."

"She's what?"

"Pregnant."

"By who?"

"Jahaad."

"Jahaad," I said surprised. I knew we weren't together any longer, but still—pregnant. I didn't exactly know how to feel about that. It wasn't like Jahaad acknowledged me anymore, but still . . . pregnant. "Whatever," I waved my hand. "Who cares?"

"That doesn't bother you?" Naja looked at me.

"Girl, please. Do I seemed concerned?" I said as I pressed the buzzer for the bus to stop.

"No, you seem ai'ight. But me, humph," she said as we stepped off the bus, "I would be pissed."

"Well, I guess that's you," I snapped. "Whatever."

Naja shook her head. "Well, at least she don't have no hee-bee-gee-bees."

"Yeah, right?" I laughed. "She could have the cooties."

"I know!" Naja laughed. "Right!"

"Played-out asses!" I said and we cracked up even more, as we reached the school's double doors.

"They are so retarded," Naja said as we walked in. But instantly the entire hallway was quiet, with the exception of Samantha and Mecca, who were laughing with Ciera and Jahaad.

I looked at Naja. "I told you they were two-faced."

"Why is everybody so quiet and staring at us?" she asked as we walked quietly down the hall.

"I don't know, but what the heck are all these?" I snatched one of the thousand pieces of paper that lined the hallway walls. Naja followed suit and we started reading the article together:

> R&B sensation Haneef is dating a young local girl, Elite Parker, whose mother is a crack addict and often leaves Elite and her sisters and brothers home alone.
>
> "Elite lied to everybody at school," Mecca, a fellow classmate said. "I doubt if Haneef even knows her real name."
>
> "I heard she slept with everyone," Samantha, another classmate, added.

> "There were times when I even paid her rent," Jahaad, Elite's ex-boyfriend, stated.

I fell against my locker. I couldn't believe this was happening. I looked around and everyone except Naja—who'd walked over to Mecca and Samantha and started cursing them out—was laughing. I felt like grabbing my bags and running out, but I knew if I did that, these chickens would think they had the best of me. So although I wanted to leave, and I had to get the hell out of there, I couldn't just bolt through the doors like a bat out of hell. I had to serve these fools first, and then I could leave and cry in peace.

I walked over and stood by Naja. "I got this boo-boo," I said to Naja, loud enough for everyone who wanted a show to know they were about to get one. "Let me just shut all y'all down real quick. Every last one of y'all either tryna be me—or tryna get with me—" Then I turned to Jahaad and said, "So you really think I give a damn about whatever lie you sold some punk ass paper? What, you jealous, 'cause Haneef don't want y'all crab-infested jump-off behinds?! Look at you, talkin' about who's a crackhead. Who get high and drunk more than you two?"

Then I pointed to Mecca and Samantha and said, "Don't say shit to me ever again! And Ciera, word you a ho and everybody knows it. What, you think you got a prize with Jahaad? Mr. Itty Bitty?!

Girl, please, lose yo'self. Matter fact—" I turned to Naja as I felt the tears hiding behind my eyes ready to buckle—"I got more important things to do. I'm outta here. Call me later." I kissed her on both cheeks, threw up a peace sign, and sashayed out the door.

I was thanking God I saw the bus was coming as soon as I stepped out of school, though I knew it wasn't the right bus to get me home. Actually, this bus was headed to New York City, but I didn't care. I needed to get someplace where I could shrink and disappear.

By the time I stepped on the bus, tears had escaped down my face. I paid my fare and made my way to the back, thanking God again that the bus wasn't crowded. I walked to the back, crouched in a corner seat, held my head down, and silently cried myself into oblivion.

When I looked up, the driver announced the last stop and pulled into Penn Station. I wiped my face, got out of my seat, and exited the bus.

I wandered around for about an hour, wondering mostly what I was going to do with my life, especially now that I'd been exposed. I had nothing. And yeah, I had a rich and famous boyfriend, but what did it mean if he didn't even know the truth?

I continued to walk a few blocks more and then my cell phone rang. "Hello?"

"Elite." It was Haneef. "Where are you?"

"Why? What you wanna do, break up with me?"

“No,” he said. “All I wanna do is talk to you about what I read in *Hip-Hop Weekly* today. I’ve been screening calls all morning. Everyone is asking me if this is true.”

“Why, it’ll mess up your image, is that it? Know what, Haneef”—I looked at the billboard poster of his CD cover—“let me make this easy for you. It’s over. I’ll catch you around.” And I hung up.

Immediately my phone rang. “What?!” I screamed and immediately attracted a group of onlookers.

“Don’t run away from me. Where are you?”

I sighed. “In the city.”

“Come see me.”

“Haneef—did you hear me? I said we were over.”

“Naja, you don’t believe that.”

He was right. I didn’t believe that. “Okay, Haneef. I’m on my way.”

“Don’t lie to me.”

“I’m not.”

I hailed a cab and twenty minutes later I was at Haneef’s apartment. I thought about what I would tell him, because I knew if I told him the truth, he would want to know why I’d lied to him the whole time. A question I couldn’t really answer.

I told security who I was and they rang Haneef to let him know I was there. By the time I got to his apartment, I felt like a scared little girl. And I hadn’t felt like that in a long time, because for the longest while, I always felt grown.

While I was standing at his door, I was determined to tell him, "Look, this is my life. Either take it or leave it." At least I was determined to do that until he opened the door and pulled me into his embrace.

I was trying to speak, but my tears muffled my voice to the point where all that could be heard were my sobs.

"Shhhh . . ." Haneef said, closing the door behind me. "Stop crying."

"But . . ."

"Shhhh . . . we'll talk about this later." He kissed me and I kissed him back. We continued to kiss passionately and before I could tell Haneef to stop, or before I could decide if I wanted him to stop, he was undressing me and I was undressing him . . .

SPIN IT . . .

Track 20

When I awoke, the sun was shining brightly in my face, and that's when I realized I'd been at Haneef's all night. Immediately my heart thundered in my chest.

"Haneef." I shook him as he lay next to me in bed. "I gotta get up."

"Ai'ight," he threw his arm over my waist. "In another hour."

"No, now." I shook my head, feeling tears knocking at the back of my eyes. "You don't understand! I have to leave. My brother and sisters are alone!"

"Isn't your mother home, Elite?"

"No!"

He sat up and pressed his back against the headboard. "Tell me the truth—and don't lie to me. Is your mother recovered, like you told me and the reporters yesterday?"

Silence.

"Why do you keep lying to me!" he screamed at me while shaking my shoulders. "Tell me the truth! That's the only way I can see how to help you!"

"I don't need your help! I can do this on my own!"

"Elite, you're only seventeen!"

We were in a screaming match. "So! What does that mean? I've always taken care of my brothers and sisters. I'm the oldest, and when my mother got on drugs so bad that she was selling the food out our house, it was me who forged her signature to get a job. It was me who went to all their plays. Me who paid for their school pictures. Me who took care of them when they were sick, and signed their report cards. Me! I told you before I've always been grown, so I need to go because they need me. Please, take me home."

Haneef wrapped his arms around me and squeezed me. I pushed against his chest. "Let me go."

"No." He squeezed tighter.

"Haneef, please," I cried. "Let me go."

"I wanna help you."

"No, I can do this."

"Elite, I care so much about you. Come on, please let me do this with you."

"You care that much about me?"

"Look," he said as he pushed my hair away from my face, "remember when I told you my mother worked all the time and I was always with my brothers?"

"Yeah."

"Well, it was because my mother was on drugs. She got high and so did my dad."

"Really?"

"Yeah."

"I never heard that."

"Because I was embarrassed, but not anymore. If it means helping you, then I'll give interview after interview. But you can't go through this alone, because you are not alone."

"Did they . . . do they . . ."

"What? Still get high?"

"Yeah."

"No. They got help. Both of them went to rehab and now they're clean. They have a lot of programs for addicts here in the city. They can help your mother if she wants to be helped. But she has to want to be helped."

"I'll tell her."

"No, she has to want to."

"But I want her to get clean."

"But she has the drug problem, not you."

I sat silently. I'd never thought of that. I knew I didn't get high, but I still felt like . . . I needed to get help. But for the first time in my life, I realized my mother was the only one who could stop herself from getting high.

SPIN IT . . .

Track 21

It was six in the morning and I realized that the more days that passed, the more my life was coming apart at the seams. I always thought I would have it all together, and that no matter what, I'd be able to take care of my brothers and sisters. But with Ny'eem in jail, I felt like all I did was fail. Especially since whenever he called the house and told me how badly he wanted to come home, the only thing I could do was cry.

I got out of bed, woke the twins and Mica, got us all ready for school, dropped them off, and returned to hell's dungeon, also known as Arts High. As I approached the entrance, I saw one of the flyers from *Hip-Hop Weekly*, which spilled my life's secrets, being whipped along the sidewalk by the wind. I started to grab it and rip it to shreds but I didn't, because at that moment—true story—I didn't even care.

"Elite!" Naja said, running up behind me. "You all right?"

"Yeah," I said somberly. "I'm straight."

"We gon' return those clothes tonight?" she asked as we headed to class.

"Yeah, I think we need to."

I was quiet most of the day, other than saying what I had to to my teachers about my schoolwork.

A few hours later, when school ended, Naja and I headed to work. Thelma was nowhere to be found, and the crew who had worked the shift before us had left as soon as we arrived.

"And you're so quiet because . . . ?" Naja said as we slyly returned the clothes we'd been "borrowing."

"No reason," I said. "But you know I'm not doing this anymore." I turned and gave her emphasis with my eyes. "This stealing and shit is not for me. And another thing, like . . . we never really got to talk about it, but that going out to the club and getting drunk was not cool."

"Don't you think I know that?" she snapped. "Heck, I'm the one on lockdown forever."

"And you got what your hand called for, too." I handed her a plastic hanger, for her next outfit. "You need to calm down, Naja, and stop giving into peer pressure—"

“Peer pressure. Excuse you, Grandma,” she said sarcastically.

“Call me whatever. Do you know you can die from drinking too much? Like, do you really understand that a lot of people could have gotten into trouble if you had been caught drinking?”

“Elite, but—”

“No buts, ’cause I’m so serious, Naja. You need to get it together, for real. Because I’m not going along with that craziness anymore, ai’ight. So whether it’s ‘borrowing clothes’ or ‘getting drunk at the club,’ count me out.”

“You really mean that?”

“Yes, look—I’ve had drugs and shit ruining my life, which is why I try to stay away from them. And I don’t want the people I love gettin’ high, drunk, or having to go through anything that I have. Which is why I’m saying, all of this”—I waved my hand over the clothes—“is a wrap for Elite Juliana Parker.”

“Awwl, Elite, you love me?” she gave me a goofy smile.

“Of course I do. We’re best friends, but if you try that shit you did at the club, our friendship is a wrap.”

“Whatever,” she laughed. “But as far as this ‘borrowing clothes’ stuff, I can’t handle the pressure either, especially with Thelma suspicious.”

“That’s exactly what I’m saying.”

It took us an hour to return everything, and as

we placed the last item on the rack, Thelma and two male customers walked in. "Elite, Naja," she said sternly, "I need to see you."

"Now?" I said. "Or when we are about to close?"

"Now. Right now."

Naja sighed. "Thelma, if we leave no one will be watching the floor."

"Oh," Thelma said snippy. "I have someone watching the floor at all times."

"If you say so," Naja said as we followed Thelma to the back of the boutique. I noticed the men, who I thought had been customers, were coming behind her.

"Who are they?" Naja mumbled under her breath.

"I don't know," I mumbled back.

"Excuse me, Thelma. What's going on?" I asked her while looking at the men suspiciously.

"You two have been stealing from here," Thelma said without hesitation, "and I am pressing charges."

"Huh?" Naja and I said simultaneously with surprise. My heart thundered in my chest and immediately my throat clogged. But then again, maybe I heard wrong. "What did you say, Thelma?"

"Don't try and lie!"

"Lie about what?" Naja protested.

"Stealing!"

"Huh?" Naja and I said simultaneously again.

"Don't huh me," Thelma snapped. "I was so hurt and disappointed when I found this out, I absolutely couldn't believe it was you two. But then you tried to take the tape out . . ." She shook her head in disgust.

"Thelma—"

"Be quiet, because you're about to lie."

"I wasn't."

"Stop it! Because what you didn't know is that there is a backup tape. Where I was able to see the whole thing." She looked at me with tears in her eyes. "I'm really disappointed in you two. I thought you were the best workers I had. And Elite, you were the assistant manager. Why would you do this?"

I started to tell her that it was because I was stupid, but quickly changed my mind.

"It wasn't Elite," Naja said. "It was me. Don't arrest her, arrest me."

"Naja," I said and jerked my neck in surprise. "It wasn't just you. It was both of us."

"No, it was my idea."

"Whoever's idea," Thelma interrupted, "it doesn't matter. You can figure that out when you get to court, but you're both being arrested."

"Thelma—" I attempted to speak to her again.

"I don't want to hear it."

"Let me explain—"

"Explain it to the judge!" she said as the men, who we soon discovered were Short Hills police officers, grabbed us by the wrists and twisted our arms behind our backs. Naja started to scream and cry, while tears rolled silently down my cheeks. It's no way life got any worse than this.

"You have the right to remain silent . . ." The officers read us our rights while handcuffing us. Afterwards, they escorted us out the back entrance of the mall to their police car, where we were pushed into the backseat.

Handcuffed and on our way to the precinct, I looked out the window and stared at the reflection of myself. I knew stealing was wrong, but I never thought I would get arrested. I had no idea what I was gonna do because, unlike Naja, I didn't have a mother and father who would come and pick me up.

Once we arrived at the police station, we were placed on a wooden bench, handcuffed to it by one hand, and instructed to use the other hand to call our parents. If they didn't come get us within the hour, we'd be hauled to downtown Newark to the Youth House.

Tears filled my eyes as I stared at the phone, 'cause I didn't have even one number to call.

"I'ma—I'ma—" Naja stuttered, "die."

"Would you stop crying so loud?" I looked at her like she was crazy. "But then again, keep it up and maybe they'll put us out for being cry babies."

"You cracking jokes. I'm about to die, and you're telling jokes."

"That sounded like a joke to you? Please. But what happened to you being all tough?"

"I was okay until they put handcuffs on me . . . now I want my mommy." She began to wail again. "My mother and father gon' kick my ass. They raised me better than this. And here I am, disgracing the family."

"Naja—"

"My mother," she sobbed, "my mother . . . she already told me I was lucky to have survived the car situation, and now this."

"At least you have someone to call. Please, my mother is out roaming the streets."

Naja was silent for a moment, then wailed even louder. "We both jacked up. . . . awwl! Lawd, help us. I'm sorry, Elite. We in a hot mess! Why couldn't Thelma just have us do the dishes. What happened to those days?"

"Naja, please," I said as she nervously picked up the phone and called her parents. "Mommy—Mommy," she stuttered. "I have something to tell you!"

"What?" I heard Neecy scream through the phone.

"They may be putting me on death row. Life as we know it," she wailed, "awwll no! Jeeeeeesussssss! Life as we know it may never be the same. I love you," she continued to cry. "Fight for world peace, fight against hunger, vote for Obama, and be strong for me."

God, how I wanted to smack her in the back of her head. "Ask them to come get you, fool!"

"Oh, yeah"—she wiped her eyes—"can you come

and get me from the Short Hills police station? We got into a li'l itty bitty situation."

"What?" I heard Neecy scream.

"Don't panic, Ma." Naja had the nerve to try and reassure somebody. "It's not what you think. Thelma just didn't like us borrowing clothes from the boutique and not exactly telling anyone."

I could've sworn the phone flew off Naja's ear, because all I heard was a buncha screaming and Neecy saying over and over again, "You just wait 'til I see you!"

When Naja hung up, she shook her head.

"What did she say?"

"She said that tonight may be the night she gives me up for adoption."

"Well, hell." I placed my chin in the palms of my hands. "I know I'm doomed then."

This had to be the worst, especially since I didn't know what my fate would be. At least Naja had someone to call. Me, well I would have to deal with whatever came my way.

"Where are they at?" soon screamed its way through the precinct.

"You go ahead on home," Naja said, "and pretend you're me. I'ma just chill out here for a li'l while."

"Naja!" her mother screamed. "I'ma beat the junk out of you!"

"Neecy!" her father snapped. "You gots to chill." Then he looked at Naja and said, "I'ma whup yo' ass!"

Dang, I ain't never heard him say that before.

"Naja!" Neecy screamed. "You hear me talking

to you?"

"You have reached . . ." Naja said, sounding like a computerized operator, "a number that is no longer in service."

"Oh, now you out of order?! Yo' ass shoulda been outta order when you and Elite were up there at ya job stealing those clothes. I promise you I won't leave neither one of y'all alone in my house anymore! Buncha skutter-buttah thieves! And here Mom-Mom was watching TV and said somebody who looked like you two robbed a bank she owned. Now I'm really starting to think it may have been you two."

"Ma'am," one of the officers said. "Which one are you coming to get?"

"Both of them," she snapped.

I blinked in disbelief.

"They're both your daughters?"

"Yeah."

After Neecy signed a few papers, Naja and I were released. Naja was visibly shaken, while I was just relieved to be getting out of there.

As we drove, Neecy continued to go off, some of it I heard and some of it I didn't. "Maybe you two," she said as we pulled in front of my building, where I noticed there were fire engines, "don't need to be best friends. Cause every time you're together, something horrible happens."

I was too busy trying to figure out what the fire

engines were doing, and why I could've sworn I heard Mica crying, yet couldn't find him, to pay much attention to what Neecy had to say.

I didn't even acknowledge her statement. Instead I got out of the car and walked toward the entrance of my building. "Elite," Neecy said as she and Naja walked behind me. "What is going on here?"

"I don't know."

"Well, we gon' find out." She grabbed me by my hand and led me into the building, where I spotted two social workers, taking the twins and Mica with them.

"What's going on?" I yelled, tears bubbling in my eyes.

"Are you Elite?"

"Yes."

"Well, you have to come with us."

"And why is that? And where are you taking these children?" Neecy demanded to know.

Mica and the twins were crying and screaming at the top of their lungs, trying to reach for me, but the social worker held them back.

"Let me talk to them!" I yelled.

"Calm down," one social worker insisted.

"I'm not calming nothing down! Let me talk to them."

She allowed them to come to me and they all ran, hugging my legs. Neecy started talking to the social workers while I wiped my brother and sisters' tears and asked them, "What happened?"

“You were late,” Aniyah cried.

“And we thought you weren’t coming back,” Sydney added.

“So I asked Aniyah to cook me something to eat,” Mica said sadly, “and she did. But it was only a small fire, nothing big.”

“But it could’ve been worse!” one of the social workers chimed in. “Now, can you tell us where your mother is?”

“I don’t know.” I looked at her. “I really don’t.”

“Well, since Deniece Jones here said you could stay with her, we have to take your brother and sisters to a foster home.”

“What?” I was in disbelief.

“Here.” She handed me a card. “Have your mother call the office first thing in the morning.”

I couldn’t believe it, but I tried to be as strong as I could. “Listen,” I said to Mica and the twins, “everything will be okay. You listen to what the ladies say and be on your best behavior.”

“I don’t wanna go!” they cried.

“And I don’t want you to go, but you have to. Okay?”

“Yes,” they cried. “Are we gon’ see you again?”

A lump filled my throat as I realized the answer to that question was that I didn’t know. “Yes,” I said to them, holding my tears back. “You will.”

I stood up straight and as I watched them leave, I felt as if someone was slicing my heart out, and just when I thought things couldn’t get any worse, I realized the world had ended. I wasn’t sure if my feet were moving as I followed Neecy out of the building and watched my sisters and brother leave in the back of a state car. I didn't know how I was living and breathing because my heart had fallen out.

Neecy placed her arm around my shoulders and I completely fell apart. I felt Naja's hand on my back, rubbing it, as if she were trying to make me feel better, but at that moment I didn't think that anything ever would.

As we headed back to the car, I felt like we'd stepped into a sea of flashing cubes, as reporters were taking my picture, sticking microphones in my face, and asking me questions.

STUCK

My whole world was spinning. I had a headache, and I felt like I might just curl up and die. It was like . . . I wanted to cry but I didn't know how to cry. Even though when I don't want to cry, I can't make myself stop. I had been sitting in the middle of my apartment floor for hours, with my knees pulled to my chest, listening to the echo of my own voice or the sighing of my own breath, not understanding why this was happening to me. All I wanted to do was take care of my sisters and brothers, and somehow in the midst of all of it, be a teenager, too.

But my pain wasn't about me being a teenager, it was about me disappointing Ny'eem, Mica, Aniyah, and Sydney. They'd depended on me, and look what I'd done.

I held my head down and cried into the fold of

my knees until tears filled my eyes and snot clogged my nose.

An hour into wondering exactly when I'd died and gone to hell, I heard a key turning in the door, my mother laughing, and Gary saying, "Hur' up, I gotta pee."

I continued to hold my head down as I wiped my face.

"Elite," my mother called to me as I heard Gary run toward the back. "Why you sittin' there?"

I held my tear-stained face up and looked her directly in the eyes. All sorts of nasty things to spit at her ran through my mind, but instead of slapping her with what I really wanted to say, I sat quietly and watched her look around the room. "Where the kids?"

I just shook my head.

"Elite? You hear me talking to you?"

Silence.

She walked over and stood directly in front of me. "Why are you crying?" She walked away from me and started roaming the apartment. She threw open all the doors and started calling their names, "Aniyah, Mommy's home. Mica, come 'mere. Syd!" She repeated herself, "Aniyah, Mommy's home. Mica, come 'mere. Syd!" Tears formed in her eyes. "Lee-Lee, where the babies?"

I stood up and squinted. "Babies?" I couldn't believe she said that. "'Lee-Lee, where are the babies?'" I turned my head from side to side in disbelief. "'Where are the babies?' How about this:

where you been? Where's their mother? Where's she at? Getting high, sucking a glass pipe? Being a junkie in the hallway, in the street, running off with some scallywag ass bum—"

"Excuse you?" Gary said as he came out of the bathroom. "What you say?"

"Scallywag ass bum!" I jerked my neck so hard, it was a wonder I didn't spit in their faces. Tears were threatening to spill down my cheeks again, but I was determined not to cry. "Huh, Ma?! 'Where are the babies?' For the last eight years, you haven't had no dang babies. All you had was some rock! I had the babies. I had them. You have done nothing but run the streets and leave us here to fend for ourselves. Do you know how many nights we went to bed hungry, crying, wet, wondering where you were? Babies?! Do you even know them? Do you know their favorite color, what they like, their favorite television show? Do you know why Mica dresses in that stupid ass sheet? Because he thinks that Superman is the only one that can save you, and that's what he wants to become—Superman! All of this for you. Do you know I was arrested for stealing? And instead of being able to call you, Naja's mother had to come and get me? Do you know anything about me? Do you even think about Ny'eem, who's locked up and can't come home until you are able to take custody of him, and you knew that, and what—what has changed about you? I'll tell you what has changed. The time of the day—nothing else—and if anything, you've gotten worse!

"So you wanna know where your babies are? They're in foster care, where they're going to be adopted because you don't know how to be a mother. All you know how to be is a junkie!"

No matter how hard I tried to hold them back, tears poured down my face to the point where they were blinding me.

My mother stood there in shock. I'd never seen her look like this. Almost as if she'd seen a ghost, or better yet, was going to kick my butt. But the way I felt, I was willing to take on the challenge. I didn't care anymore. I really didn't. I had nothing, and she had even less than that.

She leaned against the wall beside where I was standing and slid to the floor. She pulled her knees and cried into the folds. I just looked at her. I wanted to hold her and hug her and tell her everything was going to be alright. But this time I couldn't . . . because honestly I didn't know what being alright was anymore.

I turned around, walked toward the front door, and slammed it behind me.

SPIN IT . . .

Track 22

For the next two days I was a zombie. Haneef called me a million times but not once did I answer the phone. I'm not sure if I was embarrassed, or I simply wasn't feeling it anymore. Truthfully, I couldn't tell if I was coming or going and really, I'm not sure I cared. I felt like . . . like, everything was lost. What had happened to the mornings where I would wake up and get everybody together, and yeah, maybe, deep down we all missed our mother and wished she was there, but I did what I had to do.

I really thought I had it together, but . . . I had nothing to show for it . . . nothing . . .

I turned over on my side, looked at Naja's wall that was covered with pictures we'd taken in downtown Newark in front of a spray painted backdrop which read Brick City, and cried myself to sleep.

"Elite." I felt someone lightly shake my hip and when I turned over, I realized it was Neecy.

"Yes." I rubbed my eyes.

"Someone's here to see you."

"Okay." I stretched, slid on my slippers, and dragged myself to the living room, where my mother was standing in the same clothes she had on two days ago, and her eyes looked as if she'd been crying that long.

I shook my head, looked toward the ceiling, and sucked my teeth. "Yeah," I said, feeling an iron fist clog my throat. I was warring inside, trying to keep tears from falling from my eyes. "What do you want?" I snapped.

"How you doin'?" She nervously leaned from one foot to the next.

"Psst," I frowned. "What, I need to tell you again how I'm doing? You didn't get it the last time we spoke? What'd you do? Get high and forget?"

"Lee-Lee," she said, shocked.

"My name is Elite. Remember, you named me that," I said sarcastically, "because you thought I was destined—or whatever that mess was you said—to be the best."

"It wasn't mess."

"Oh, yeah," I grimaced. "I guess I was the best kid a crackhead could have. Hmph, seems we found something you did right."

"Don't speak to me like that!" she snapped as tears formed in her eyes.

"Please." I waved my hand as if I could care

less. "Get on with it, what are you here for?!" I flopped down on the couch and crossed my arms. My stomach was doing backflips and for the first time in my life, I felt like if I never saw my mother again, it would be fine.

"Listen, I don't expect you to understand, but I have a lot of problems and things I've had to deal with that have nothing to do with you or your sisters and brothers."

"Yeah . . ." I crooked my neck. "I couldn't tell."

"Let me finish," she said. I could tell I was trying her patience. "I have some plenty ugly things," she continued, "that have happened in my life, and I didn't know . . . I really didn't know how to deal with them, so I turned to drugs—"

"Yeah, and ruined our lives."

"I know that—I've always known that I wasn't a good mother, so I kept running away from reality. My reality, your reality, our reality. So to medicate and feel better, I stayed gone for days at a time. I got high—"

"So we're to blame for you getting high?" I couldn't believe this.

"No, that's not what I'm saying. I'm saying that I'm the mother and I never acted like one. I've done some things I'm not proud of. And maybe this is what it took, the twins and Mica in foster care, Ny'eem in jail, and you hating me. Maybe I needed this so that I could see how much help I really need."

My throat was trembling; her saying this was

the last thing I expected. Tears were clouding my eyes to the point where I could no longer see.

"And that's what I've decided to do. Get some help."

"Uhm hmm," was all I could say as I wiped my tears away. I was doing all I could to act tough, like I didn't care, but for some reason my emotions were defeating me.

"And I know you may never understand and you may never forgive me . . . and I'm not sure I even deserve your forgiveness or your love, but I'm determined to get some help, and this time, I'm getting help for me. No one else but me, and I can only pray that one day we'll be mother and daughter again."

She stood there and stared at me as if she were expecting me to clap, run into her arms, or say that I understand or something, but instead I let my silence speak for me. I stood up from the sofa, wiped my face again, went into Naja's room, and slammed the door.

After replaying the argument I had with my mother over in my head at least a thousand times, I heard a soft knock on the door. "Elite."

"Yes."

"May I come in?"

"Yes."

Neecy walked into the room and pointed to the bed. "You mind," she said as she sat down on the edge of the bed, "if I speak to you for a minute?"

"No, not at all."

"Good, 'cause I wanna talk to you about something." She grabbed my hands and placed them between hers. Then she gave me a sly smile and closed one eye playfully. "Look, I try not to be nosy, but sometimes I am."

I laughed a little, especially since I knew she was beyond nosy.

"And I just want you to listen, okay?"

"Okay."

"I think you should really think about some of the things your mother said to you today, because I believe that she means it—"

"You don't know—"

"I said listen," she said as she placed her index finger against my lips.

"I know she may have done some things to hurt you and maybe I don't know what it's like to have a mother on drugs, but I do know what it's like to have a father who's an alcoholic. Ever since I could remember, my father drank." She closed her eyes as if she were fighting off a bad memory. "And he drank and he drank, and he drank so much that I often wondered if he knew who and where he was half of the time. And I'll tell you, Elite, he did some pretty bad things."

"Really?"

"Yes. He would cuss us out, accuse me and brothers of things, you name it—he said we did it. And it took many, many years for him to realize he had a problem, and when he did, I wanted nothing to do with him."

"You didn't?"

"No, and when he came to me to apologize and seek my forgiveness, do you know what I did?"

"What? Forgave him?"

"No. I told him I never wanted to see him again, that I hated him, and to get out of my life."

"I know how you feel," I said more to myself than to her.

"I'm sure you do, but not long after he came and apologized to me, he died, and I never got a chance to tell him that I forgave him. That I loved him and was only angry with him. I was hurt and I wanted to hurt him the same way he'd hurt me."

"So," I asked, scared of what her answer might be, "did you ever stop hurting?"

"Well . . . over the years, it's gotten better and I've learned to live with it, but who knows what would've happened had I forgiven him. Maybe the hurt would have gone away. But now I'll never have a chance to undo my telling him to get out of my life. You understand what I'm saying to you?"

"Yes. I guess . . . I never thought of it that way."

She rose off the bed. " Well, maybe you should. Now while you get some rest, think about what I said. You've had a hard couple of days, but around here, I may let you miss one day of school, but two in a row is a no-no. Feel me?" she teased.

I laughed. "Yes, ma'am. I feel you."

SPIN IT . . .

Track 23

Going to school was getting harder by the day. The very people who faked their way into my life because I was dating Haneef were the same ones who kept talking crap about me. I heard a thousand different spins on my life: her mother's a crackhead—no, it's her father; her sisters and brothers are adopted—no, she's adopted. They're in foster care—no, they live on the streets . . . and on it went. I couldn't wait for the last day of school, so I could decide if I even wanted to come back.

Naja insisted I ignore them, which I did, but it still didn't make it hurt any less. I'd been trying to ignore Haneef because I was too embarrassed, and I really didn't know what to say to him. So I gave up and wished somehow I could just rewind time, and go back to when he was simply a poster on my ceiling.

"Elite!" Naja ran after me down the hall as the lunch bell rang. "Let's go in the cafeteria."

"Naja," I said, "I don't know about that."

"What? What don't you know?"

"If we should do that. I mean, if you wanna go, you go ahead. I might go hang out in the library."

"Girl, would you come on. Forget the haters."

Reluctantly, I went into the lunch room and stood in line. I felt like all eyes were on me as soon as I walked in. I could see some people staring and pointing as I fixed my tray and we walked toward one of the tables.

"This shit is crazy," I said to Naja. "Like for real, none of them even know the truth about what's going on. It's like I'm dating Usher or some shit. I think I know how Maneka feels."

Naja snickered. "You're nothing like Maneka, so please."

I laughed. "Maybe I should call Haneef and have him go on TV and defend me, like Usher did."

"Yeah, and look stupid. But anyway, when's the last time you heard from Haneef?"

"He calls me at least a hundred times a day, but I haven't answered the phone."

"Why?" She looked confused.

"Because I've been thinking about breaking up with him."

"Are you serious? Because of this stuff?"

"Yeah . . . it's too much. The reporters, people all in my business, and all the lies."

"Excuse you, Elite, but you started the lies. He didn't."

"She's always lying from what I hear," floated over my shoulder and into my conversation. I turned around and it was Ciera—and if it wasn't for the baby in her stomach, I would've jabbed her. "You better go 'head, Ciera."

"You don't tell me what to do."

"That's right," Jahaad said as he walked over. "You don't tell my wifey what she better do."

Ciera blushed and I snapped, "I didn't tell her what she better do, but I'ma tell you that you better get the hell out my face!"

"Or what, Elite?" Jahaad said as if he were daring me.

"Or I'ma catch you in it!" I snapped my neck as Naja stood beside me like a soldier, ready to attack.

"And then I'ma follow up," she said.

"Man, please," Jahaad spat and waved his hand. "Elite, you must not remember who you talking to. You know I know your mother has always been on drugs, and that you ain't never been all that you thought you were. And now because you dating some played-out rap dude, you think you all that and a bag of chips, but I can't tell with your life blowing up in the papers every day."

"Tell her ass, baby," Ciera spat.

"Tell me what?" I pointed my finger in their

face. "You 'spose to be thugged out, but right now you sounding like a li'l girl. My six-year-old brother got more heart than you. You're a joke! What, you looking for me to laugh in your face? Psst, mofo, please. Both y'all look stupid. A set of damn creeps and losers. No wonder you two got together. What, you think," I pointed to Ciera, "that you accomplished something by being with this dude? He's ridiculous, and he's mad because he knows I know how long he's really been played."

"You just saying that because you tryna get back with me."

"Boy, please, who you talking to? We both know that's nowhere near true. You know I don't want you and never have, and then you with this chick. Spare me. You're nothing. Listen to your names together: Jahaad and Ciera. Hell, it sounds like trash."

"I can't believe you said that!" Ciera barked.

"Whatever—" I gave Naja a fist bump—"either go hard or go home. Otherwise, you being in my face is wasted space. So, my suggestion to you is to bounce."

Naja hunched her shoulders and flicked her hands. "Guess she told yo' ass."

"You lucky I'm pregnant," Ciera spat. "Otherwise, it would be on."

"Well, come see me when you're not so I can kick your ass and get this over with."

The entire cafeteria was laughing and shaking their heads as Jahaad and Ciera walked away, talking trash. But whatever, as long as they kept it movin', I didn't care what they said. "You wanna leave?" Naja asked, pointing to the clock. "It's not that much time left."

"No, we gon' finish our lunch," I insisted. "I'm gettin' a little tired of runnin'. Hmph, I go to school here, too."

After lunch, Naja and I went back to class and although there were a few whispers and fingers pointing, I tried my best to ignore them. I had other things to worry about, like when I was going to see Mica and the twins again, when Ny'eem was getting out of jail, getting a job, and what I was going to do about my relationship with Haneef.

Once the school day ended, Naja and I walked to the bus stop together. "Elite!" I heard someone yell my name and when I looked up, it was Haneef, leaning against the back door of his Hummer. "Come here."

I sucked my teeth. "Naja, go tell him I'm not coming."

"Nope," she said as the oncoming bus came. "You need to talk to him and I'm going home, so I'll see you then. Bye." She smiled and waved.

I watched as Naja dropped her change in the money collector and the bus doors closed. I stood there and sighed as the bus rode away and I was left there staring at Haneef, who melted my resistance every time I saw him.

"All I wanna know is what did I do?" Haneef asked.

I looked at him surprised. I couldn't believe he was asking me what he did? He didn't do anything. It was me who lied and made up this stupid ass life that was blowing up in my face. Me, not him. He was always honest. I was the one who lied about everything. He was perfect . . . and I was . . . a mess. I walked over to where he was, and into his embrace.

"I know it's not easy being with me. The reporters and the nasty rumors on top of everything you're going through at home. But, Elite, you're too special for me to just bounce and let you push me away."

"But, Haneef," I sniffed.

"I'm not walking away, Elite. No matter what you say, you can forget about it."

"But I'm like . . . bad for your image."

"That's not your concern. Now can we get in the car and talk about this?"

"Yes."

As the driver pulled off into traffic, Haneef pushed a button and the black-tinted divider came up and gave us more privacy. "Why haven't you been returning any of my calls?"

"Because," I said, "I just didn't know what to say. My life is a mess. You know, my brother is in jail and my sisters and brother—" Tears trembled in my throat.

"Are where?"

"In foster care. And my job, I lost it."

"What?" he said in shock.

"Didn't you read it in the paper?"

"I saw some of it, but honestly I try not to read that garbage too much. In this business, you have to have thick skin."

"I guess, but my life is a mess and I feel lost." I intentionally left out the details of why I was fired. I was too embarrassed to admit what I'd done.

"Li'l Ma, you don't have to deal with this alone. Have you spoken to your mother?"

"Barely. She tried to apologize, but I didn't want to hear it. She claims she's going to be getting help."

"Look, this isn't the end of the world. Things can change."

"You think so?"

"Yes."

"But how do you know."

"Because when I was a kid, I went through the same things."

SPIN IT . . .

Track 24

I woke up the next morning with the sun in my face and the determination to never cry or feel sorry for myself again. I've known it forever: nothing changed through moaning and complaining. And yeah, for a hot minute, I was slippin', but I was cool. Enough was enough. It had been three weeks since my life had fallen apart, yet somehow and someway, I had to put it back together.

I stretched my arms toward the ceiling and as I sat up in bed, my cell phone rang. "Hello?"

"What's good, Li'l Ma?"

I looked at the clock: seven a.m. Then I looked at Naja, who was still sleeping, as I flipped my phone open. "You have no regard for time, do you?" I know Haneef could hear me smiling as I let out a slight giggle.

"Time?" he said as if he were playfully surprised. "What's that? I don't think I've ever heard of time." He laughed.

"You are so silly."

"Yeah, and you love it."

"Whatever, Big Head." I cracked up.

"Look at you trying to sound like your old self again."

"I know," I sighed. "I'm determined not to feel sorry for myself anymore. To hell with this crying and carrying on."

"Well, Li'l Ma, things happen you know, and sometimes it's okay to get down, as long as you don't stay down."

"My point exactly."

"Besides, you're way too pretty to be all upset."

I blushed. "Haneef," I whined a bit. "Would you stop?"

"You know you don't want me to stop."

I blushed again. "Anyway, so what are you doing today?" I said, changing the subject.

"I have to fly to L.A. The awards are tonight."

"Oh, that's right. So are you performing?"

"Yeah, and I wish you could be there."

"I could come with you if you want me to."

"Nah, Li'l Ma, that won't do nothing but get me in trouble," he laughed. "Plus, it's a lot of last minute stuff I have to finish up."

"Oh," I said as I tried to hide my disappointment.

"But next year, baby. I promise."

“It’s cool. I may go out with Naja and her family tonight anyway.”

“Oh, that’d be great!” he said, a little too excited. “I think you should go.”

“Oh . . . kay . . . you can calm down. You’re awfully excited to not have me there with you.”

“What? You know it ain’t even like that. It’s just some business I need to take care of. Strictly business,” he said as if he could sense how I felt. “It’s work, baby, nothing else.”

“Alright, Haneef. I understand. How long will you be away?”

“Two days, and then I’m back here in your arms.”

I was smiling so hard and so wide my cheeks started to ache. “I’ll be waiting.”

“You better be. You gon’ miss me?” he asked seriously.

“Like crazy.”

“Alright. Well give it to me.”

“What?” I laughed.

“My kiss.”

So I smacked my lips loudly into the phone.

“That’s what I’m talkin’ about.”

“Now give me one.”

“Elite—I’ma grown man, baby. What I look like blowing kisses over the phone?”

“I know you’re not telling me no.” I twisted my lips.

“Me? Tell my baby no? Never.”

"Okay, well give it to me."

He gave me a kiss over the phone and I said, "You wrong for that."

"What?"

"Did you brush your teeth?"

"Oh no, you didn't," he laughed. "You're the one just waking up."

"I'ma miss you, Haneef." I felt my heart sink into my chest.

"I'll be back, Li'l Ma, and when I come, I'ma come scoop you."

"Alright."

"Alright . . ."

We both paused, and I held on to the phone. "Hmmmm, okay baby, you hang up first," I insisted.

"Nah, I can't. You hang up. I don't like hanging up on you. You go first."

"No, you first. Hang up."

"Oh . . . my . . . God . . ." Naja lifted her head from the pillow. "What are y'all, dumb and dumber? The phone doesn't hang up like that. You have to physically do it. Just place it on the receiver and you'll disconnect the call. It works wonders."

"Shut up," I mouthed at her. "Hater."

She waved her hand dismissively at me and turned back over to sleep.

"Haneef," I said, "I'ma miss you. Call me every day."

"I will. You know I will. Now I have a plane to catch, so we're going to have to hang up."

"Okay, on the count of three."

We counted together, "One . . . two . . . three."

I held on to see if he really hung up and when I could still hear him breathing, I whispered, "Come get me as soon as you get back."

"I will," he whispered back. "I love you, Elite."

I paused. "What?" Maybe I heard him wrong.

"I love you," he said again. "Don't let nothing question that."

"I love you, too." And we both counted to three again and hung up.

"You two," Naja turned back over toward me, "are crazy. I really don't understand how you don't know how to use the phone. I could've showed you that, Elite."

"Naja, it wasn't like that. Haven't you ever not been able to hang up on your boyfriend?"

"No. Whenever I had one, he would say bye, I would say bye, and then I would never hear from him again."

"I wonder why?" I mumbled.

"What you say?"

"Nothing." I threw the covers off me and eased out of bed.

"Where are you going?"

"To find my mother. I need to talk to her."

"That's good, Elite. You think you'll find her?"

"I hope so."

"Well, if you do, invite her out to the movies with us."

"I didn't know we were going to a movie."

“Yeah, it’s Mom-Mom’s birthday. We take her to the movies once a year and it makes her think she’s having a family reunion.”

I shook my head. Naja’s whole family was crazy. They were the nicest people I knew, but they were nuts. “Y’all ain’t right.”

“No,” Naja shook her head. “You know our last name is Jones.”

That was it. I’d heard enough. I gathered my clothes for the day, showered, dressed, told Naja bye, gave her mother a kiss on the cheek and told her I’d be back, and headed out the door.

I walked down the block toward my building and hoped my mother was there. As I approached the stoop, I saw Gary sitting on the bottom step with a lit cigarette shaking from the corner of his lips.

“Hey, Lee-Lee.”

He couldn’t have expected me to speak. I walked right past him and directly into the building. I did not have time for his foolishness. Once I reached our apartment, I put my key in the lock and walked in. At first I felt eerie as memories flooded my mind and clogged my throat, creating an iron fist inside me. I did what I could to shake it off as I walked through the rooms, but saw no sign of my mother. It didn’t seem as if she’d been there in days.

I hated that I felt tears creep into my eyes, placing me in direct opposition to my newly declared constitution, but I did what I could to hold them back. I reared my shoulders back, walked out of the apartment, and locked the door. I wanted to break down, but how could I? Hadn't I asked for this? I did tell my Ma to go away . . . and maybe . . . just maybe . . . she took my advice. As I walked down the hall, I knew my tears wouldn't be staying at bay. And it didn't take long before I felt them leaving my eyes and easing down my cheeks. I wiped my face and bumped directly into Gary.

"Dang, Gary, watch where you going!"

"My bad."

He was so played. "Gary, have you seen my mother?"

"I . . ." he said as he paused and sniffed, "I . . ." He tried to speak again, and if I wasn't mistaken, he looked to be a few seconds from breaking down and crying. "I lost her . . ." he bellowed. "Lord have mercy, she played me out."

"Played you out?"

"She left me."

A smile lit up my face. "Where'd she go?"

"You smiling, Elite?" he said, taken aback. "You just laughing all up in my face, huh?"

"No—" I shook my head. "No, not at all."

"I can't believe this. My heartbreak is a joke to you? You never did like me. I'ma good man, Elite, and I loved yo' mama."

"Gary, I'm sure that somewhere, maybe in like the middle of the South African safari, you are a good man."

"Well, I'm glad you recognize that."

"Yeah . . . me, too, but where is my mother?"

"If I had my way, she'd be walking down the aisle with me, saying 'I do.'"

That thought was just nasty! "Okay . . . but where is she now, at this moment?"

"Beth Israel Hospital, in rehab. And you know, I asked her if I could go, and do you know what she said to me?" he said, answering his own question. "She said, 'Hell, no!' Not just 'no' but, 'Hell, no!' Like that get-out-my-face-you-played-out-fool kinda no. That stop-beggin'-me-for-two-dollars type no."

I tried to stop cheesin', but I couldn't help it much. "Why'd she tell you that?" I asked, trying to sound sincere.

"Because I told her Beth Israel Hospital sounded nice. Sounded real nice. Like some place real fancy and distinguished. You know, a good night's sleep on some nice white sheets and three full meals a day. Meet some new people and everything, you know what I mean? I even told her maybe we would see some people we knew and she told me—" he started to break down and cry—"hell no, she wasn't going on vacation."

"I guess that really hurt you, huh?"

"Tore me down, Elite. Tore me straight up and down to the ground down. Now what—what—Elite—what I'ma gon' do?"

"Go get some help, Gary." I couldn't believe I was saying that. "Clean yourself up, get a job, and be determined to be about something."

But I didn't say, 'and then come back for my mother.' And that was because I wanted this bum ass loser gone. I wanted to say good-bye, give him a salute, and send him on his way. "Take care, Gary." I patted him on the shoulder.

"Thanks, Elite. Thanks for wishing me well."

"Uhmm hmmm, anytime." I practically skipped away.

As I walked away from the building, I started thinking about everything that had been happening. I went in my purse and pulled out the social worker's card—I needed to see my sisters and brothers. I was sure she didn't work on the weekends, so I knew I'd have to leave her a message. The phone rang twice but to my surprise, she answered. "Hello, this is Mrs. Jameson."

"Hi, Mrs. Jameson . . ." I hesitated. "This is Elite."

"Hi, Elite. I was going to call you today."

"I didn't expect you to be in the office."

"Yes, sometimes I work on Saturdays. And I was thinking about you because I want to set up a visit for you and your siblings."

"Wow." I'm sure she could hear me smiling. "That's what I wanted to ask you. I miss them so much."

"And they miss you, too."

"Mrs. Jameson, did you know my mother was in rehab?"

"Oh, yes!" she said excited. "She started almost two weeks ago, and from what the program tells me, she's doing very well!"

"Do you know how long she'll be in there?" I asked.

"She'll be in the hospital for ninety days, and then she'll begin an outpatient program."

"Can I see her?"

"Not until she's released from the hospital."

I sighed. "That long?"

"It's not that long," she said. "But you do know, Elite, rehabilitation is life-long."

"Yes, I know."

"And drug abuse doesn't just affect and change a family, rehabilitation does, too. So when you see your mom again, she will be a changed person."

"Do you think . . . you know, that she'll really do it?"

"Yes, I think so. But ultimately it is up to your mom."

"True."

"But I also think that she loves you all very much, and can't wait to have you back home."

"I can't wait to be back home."

"And hopefully that will be soon," she said with a tone of reassurance. "Now, let me contact the foster parent and let her know I want to schedule a visit with your siblings. I'll call you in a few weeks, okay?"

"Mrs. Jameson, before you hang up, can you tell me if you've seen Ny'eem?"

"Yes, and I did ask the Youth House if you would be able to visit, but they said you had to be eighteen."

"I know, but when you see him again, can you tell him I love him?"

"Yes, I sure will."

"Thank you."

"Good-bye, Elite."

"Good-bye." I hung up the phone and no matter how I tried to fight it, tears escaped from my eyes and slid down my cheeks.

I had one more thing I needed to do, though. So I walked to the bus stop and caught the bus to the mall. Once I reached my destination, I was a little hesitant, not knowing what reaction I would get or even what I should expect. But I knew I had to do this, no matter what. I walked into bebe and Thelma was behind the counter.

"Thelma," I said quietly.

She looked up and I could tell her first instinct was to smile, but then it seemed she quickly changed her mind. "What do you want?" She picked up the security phone. "You're not supposed to be in here!"

"I know, Thelma, and I'm not going to stay long. I only came to apologize."

"Ha! I hope this is not some cheap ploy to get your job back or have me drop the charges, because it won't work."

"No," I shook my head. "No. I'm really sorry. I betrayed your trust and what I did was wrong, so I don't expect either one of those things. But you gave me a chance, and no matter what was going on in my life—or who I wanted to impress—it doesn't excuse what I did."

She swallowed as I continued, "You are a nice person and an even better manager, and you deserve to be treated with respect. I'm sorry I didn't give you all that I should've. So Thelma, I didn't come to persuade you to do something you don't want to, I simply came to let you know that I know I was wrong."

She cleared her throat. "Are you done?"

"Yes."

"Good. You may leave now."

I gave her a quick wave and left. No matter what, I felt good about what I'd done.

An hour later I was back at Naja's and she, her parents, and Mom-Mom were leaving to go out.

"Elite," Neecy said, "I was wondering when you were coming back. Are you coming with us?"

"No, I don't think so."

"Sure?" Naja said. "We're going to see the new Will Smith movie and Mom-Mom said she ain't seen Will and the kids in a long time."

"Sho' haven't," Mom-Mom interjected, "and I hope he don't bring that Jada with him or it's gon' be on like pop-pop-popcorn." She snapped her fingers, threw up a hand sign, and started rappin', "That's why they call me Delicious."

Oh-kay. I folded my lips. "Awwl, nah, I'll be just fine staying home."

"All right," Neecy said. "Well, there's plenty in the kitchen. See you when we get back."

"Oh, before I forget," Naja whispered as her parents and Mom-Mom walked toward the car. "Thelma called and said she wouldn't be pressing charges."

"Really? Who'd she tell that to?"

"Me. I was the one who answered the phone. And after she told me about the charges, she said that she didn't ever want to see our asses again."

"What?!" I said, excited. "And what did you say?"

"Hmph, I told her that could be arranged because I don't remember her seeing my ass anyway."

I cracked up laughing. "Bye, Naja, bye."

"What?"

"Nothing. I'll talk to you later."

I laughed all the way inside the house and after I stopped laughing so hard I walked toward the kitchen to pop me some popcorn. I had to love 'em, those people. I had to love 'em.

After retrieving the popcorn from the microwave, I noticed it was time for the awards show to start. I flopped on the sofa and clicked on the TV. But—Lil Wayne was with Tierra Marie? I cracked up. Plus, I saw what Jennifer Hudson had on—she was one hot mess!

As the stars continued down the red carpet, I ran in the kitchen and grabbed a cold Pepsi. I thought I heard Haneef's voice drifting from the TV, but I wasn't sure, so when I plopped back down on the couch and saw Chris Brown giving an interview, I knew I'd heard wrong. At least I thought I had, until the camera switched focus and I saw

Haneef holding hands with Deidra, walking onto the red carpet. I blinked at least a thousand times; I could've sworn I was seeing wrong.

"Haneef!" a reporter called to him. "Tell us how you feel about your hood Cinderella getting so much bad publicity?"

He grabbed Deidra and pulled her to his chest. "This is my hood Cinderella," and he kissed her on the lips. "All those things you heard in the papers were rumors. It's only one girl for me."

I sat there stunned. Suddenly all the air had once again left my body. So in disbelief was I that I grabbed the DVR remote and rewound the TV, only to see what I was hoping I hadn't seen—again.

It was a good thing I promised myself I wouldn't cry, because despite my chest caving in, I didn't have any more tears left.

I wasn't sure how it happened, but somehow the popcorn ended up all over the floor and I sat there too, balled up with my knees to my chest and my head in between, as I felt my heart explode inside my chest cavity.

SPIN IT . . .

Track 25

No one had ever told me that it would hurt like this. I had learned about everything else in school: math, reading, writing, sociology, economics, politics, sex, STDs . . . and all the other shit I needed to know, I learned at home with a drug-addicted mother or in the streets. But this—no one ever told me that love pierced your soul . . .

And it had to be love because I didn't know what the hell else to blame it on.

Haneef and Deidra's pictures were all over the internet and the newspapers. "The New Jay-Z and Beyoncé" were the headlines, and I was dismissed as a rumor, nothing more. Everything we'd shared and all that I'd confided in him had been reduced to shit. I was once again labeled a groupie who had won a radio contest and carried my prize too far. I should've known better than to think I was cut out to be with a superstar anyway. For real-for real, I was better off by myself anyway. In fact, I didn't even want a boyfriend.

I laid in bed, and all the lies I told myself with the hopes of feeling better blew up in my face and turned me into a crumbling fool. I'd gone from fierce, fly, and fabulous to a hot mumbling mess.

I'd been in bed for two days and my phone had been ringing nonstop. I knew it was Haneef, because right after his number stopped showing up, a mysterious number started popping up at all times of the day and night on my caller ID. I would've hoped he had gotten the hint. There was no way I could talk to him or ever be with him again. I'd been rejected, disappointed, and hurt enough in my life. I didn't need more.

"Elite," Naja said while standing in the bedroom doorway. "Haneef is here to see you."

"Tell him I said go away."

"You know what? I started to tell him that when I saw him walk up the stairs. But you know what? No. I'm not going to because you need to talk to him."

"You know what he did to me, Naja! You know what he did!"

"I know, Elite, and I'm not saying to take him back or be with him—"

"So then what are you saying?"

"I'm saying tell him what you have to say now. Forget later, forget go away and never come back—tell him now, because if he keeps standing in my living room, I might mess around and straight black on him!" And she stormed away.

I stared at the ceiling. My entire life had become too much. Somehow, something had happened and the universe was throwing my whole life out of whack. I got up, slipped on a pair of shorts and a tee, pulled my hair into a ponytail, and walked into the living room.

Haneef's eyes lit up when he saw me. "How you doin'?" I just looked at him. It was the second time, in the very same spot, that somebody who'd hurt me had asked me the same stupid ass question.

I squinted my eyes and looked at him. "You really wanna know how I'm doin'? Do you really?"

"Elite, listen, I need you to understand—"

"You don't need me to understand shit!" I poked him in his chest. "I don't even wanna hear it! All you do is lie. I've asked since the first time we started going together if you were with Deidra, and you said no—"

"It was the truth—"

"Nothing you say is the truth! You played the hell out of me and then you didn't even have the decency to tell me?! You do dirt but then you don't man up to it. I have to turn on the TV and see you standing there holding hands and kissing this chick, and then I'm dismissed as being absolutely nothing. Like garbage. My whole life has been exposed—ruined—"

"Don't blame all of that on me. It is not my fault that you lied—"

"Maybe not, but it is your fault that you lied."

"Elite, do you know what I risked being with you?"

"Now I was a risk?" I knew he hadn't put his hands on me, but I felt like he'd slapped me across the face.

"Hell, yeah, Elite—"

"Oh, now you calling me Elite—"

"Look, I need you to understand that when you're out there in the limelight, in the public eye, those people who don't know you don't care anything about you. All they care about is what they think. I'm not allowed to be human. I have to be fake—"

"Good, then you and Deidra should make a perfect couple, and you can get out of my face!"

"I'm not with Deidra!"

"I can't tell!"

"Because you're not listening!"

"I don't wanna hear it!"

"Elite—" Neecy walked into the living room and looked Haneef up and down. "Is everything okay?"

"Yes, ma'am. I'm sorry for being so loud."

"Okay, baby, well let me know if we got something that needs to be handled around here." And she walked backwards out of the room.

"Haneef, look—"

"Li'l Ma—"

"Save that for Deidra."

"Would you stop cutting me off—I'm trying to tell you that I love you."

“And I’m trying to tell you that I don’t care. I’m tired of trusting, of letting myself believe that people are true, of feeling that maybe I need to give this one a chance and that one a chance. No—no more chances. You and that sorry ass love you got can go back to Fakeville, where you came from, and I don’t ever want to see you again. Ever!” I ran into Naja’s room, grabbed the chain Haneef had given me, and threw it at him. He caught it before it fell to the floor.

“Elite—”

“I said leave!”

“Are you serious? You don’t want to hear anything I have to say.”

“No, nothing. Now get out.”

Haneef walked over to me and grabbed my hands. I tried to snatch them away but I couldn’t fight his grip. “I love you and I will always love you, but if you want me to bounce then I’m out.”

“You do that.”

He kissed me on my forehead. “I hope one day we can work this out.” He kissed each of my eyes and instantly tears fell out. He let go of my hands and I watched him walk out the door, get into his Hummer, and leave.

SPIN IT . . .

Track 26

School was finally over and things had totally changed for me. With the exception of Naja, I didn't really say much of anything to anyone, and for the most part all I did was go to school, go to my new job as a cashier at CVS, and back home again. Occasionally I'd visit with my sisters and brothers, but even they had grown extremely distant. I grew tired of telling them to stop talking about their foster home as if that was where they actually lived, and I grew exhausted of giving them instructions on how they better call their foster parents Mr. and Mrs. Not Mom and Dad. And after a while I just got agitated, aggravated, and defeated, so I kept going to the visits because I wanted to see Mica and the twins, but at the same time, the way I felt when the visits ended made me think about not going anymore.

While everyone in school was running around saying their good-byes, I told Naja I was working overtime and would meet her at home later. As I headed to the bus stop, I heard a horn beep and someone call my name. "Elite, over here!"

When I looked up, it was Mrs. Jameson!

"Hey," she waved. "You got a minute?"

"Yes."

She pulled to the side of the street and I walked over to her car. "I'm glad I caught up with you."

"Is everything okay?"

"Yes."

"Then why were you looking for me?"

"Because I didn't get a chance to call you yesterday, but if you have time I really would like to do a special visit with you and your family."

"I would love to see my sisters and brother but I just always feel misplaced and sad when the visits are over."

"Elite, I know it's hard. It's not easy for any child in this situation but there are families that sometimes need extra help in getting things right and getting life back in order. And your family happened to be one who needed our help."

"Yeah, but I just feel like everyone looks down on us."

"Listen, your family is special, and no one in

this world is better than anyone else. You don't worry about those other people."

"But my entire life has been played out in the papers and all over the internet. You had to know who my ex-boyfriend was."

"Guess what? It doesn't matter to me. You're special and that's all that counts. Now come on, I think you're going to be glad you came to this visit."

When we arrived at the social service office, the twins and Mica were already there. "Elite!" They ran over and hugged me tightly.

Every time I saw them, I realized how much I missed them. "Oh, I missed you guys so much."

"Elite, I wanna show you my report card!" Mica screamed. "I got all As!"

"And me, too!" Sydney screamed.

"Well, I got a few Bs but I'm still smart," Aniyah snapped.

"That's right, Aniyah!" I said. "Because I got some Bs, too. So come on and let's sit down. What's been going on with you guys?"

"Well, did Mrs. Jameson tell you about Mommy?"

I looked at Mrs. Jameson, who was standing near the doorway, and said, "Tell me what about Mommy?"

"That I'm clean now." My mother walked into the room and I couldn't believe it. She was absolutely beautiful! Her hair was cut into a one-sided bob and dyed honey-blond. She completely filled out a pair of size twelve jeans like she never had before, her skin was flawless, her eyes were clear, and she wasn't high. For the first time in a long time, she wasn't high. She was so pretty that even Mica and the twins were amazed.

"Is anyone going to give me a hug?" The twins and Mica ran to her while I sat there staring in disbelief. "Elite," she called to me.

I stood up and then I walked over slowly, practically falling in her arms. "You look beautiful! Really beautiful!"

"And I feel even better."

"Mommy, we missed you soooooo much!" Sydney said.

"And I missed you, too, more than you'll ever know. Now look, I wanna tell you something." She sat down in a chair and we gathered around her. "I know that I have done some pretty ugly things and none of that has been your fault. It was all mine. I will do my best to do everything I need to do to get you home, okay? Everything."

"Yes!" the twins and Mica screamed. I was a little more reluctant. I knew better than to think that someone had a magic wand and suddenly a perfect life would appear.

The visit lasted for about an hour and although I was happy to see my mother, I didn't say much to her. After all, it was all new to me. For seventeen years I knew how to handle the mother who stayed high all the time, but it had only been an hour, and I had no idea how to handle the mother who was sober. And I didn't dare dream because all my dreams seemed to blow up in my face.

"Okay, Mica, Aniyah, and Sydney, time to get ready," Mrs. Jameson said. "Mrs. Wilson is waiting to take you back."

After the twins and Mica said their good-byes, Mrs. Jameson said, "Give me a moment and I'll drop you two off." She excused herself from the room.

"I'm glad she left for a minute," my mother said, I guess in an attempt to make small talk.

"Yeah," was all I could think to say in response.

"Elite, I know this is all new to you, and I know the last time we saw each other it wasn't pleasant."

"Ma, I'm just—I'm just scared."

"I know you are and I'm scared, too, but I'm ready to do what I need to do to get my children home and my family back in order. I know that I have caused you a lot of pain, and when you're ready, I would like it very much if you would work on forgiving me so that we can see how we need to do this mother and daughter thing."

"I love you, Ma." I hugged her tightly. "I love you more than you'll ever know!"

"So does that mean you're ready to come home?"

"Yes! Whenever Mrs. Jameson tells me I can go home, I'm there."

"Well, how's let's say," Mrs. Jameson said while walking back into the room, "today?"

My mother and I looked at her like she was crazy, and smiles ran across both of our faces. "Today?" we both said.

"Yes. Your mother completed her inpatient program. She's in her outpatient program, and I really don't see why not."

"Ma, do you want me to come home?"

"Are you kidding me? Of course I do. I couldn't think of anything at this moment that I would want more."

We hugged tightly and although we rode in a car, I felt like we practically skipped to Naja's. We waved good-bye to Mrs. Jameson and went inside. I held on to my mother's hand like I was a five-year-old kid, and when we walked inside, Naja's dad looked at my mother and said, "Damn." Neecy slapped him across the back of his head and he said, "Nawl, what I meant to say was Yup-Yup."

"Anyway," Neecey said, "Cassie, you look fantastic!"

"Thank you," my mother said. "I really want to tell you how much I appreciate everything you've done for my daughter. You all took her in and treated her like family when you didn't have to. And I really thank you for that."

"Elite is a lovely girl. She and Naja have gotten into some things, but she's still a good kid and we love her." My mother and Neecy hugged and wiped a few tears away. "Okay, now look, I got a buncha stuff on the grill, some ice cold sodas, and some serious music out back. I don't know about you, Cassie, but I partied hard in the eighties, and I got a Salt-n-Pepa mix tape that's cold, feel me?"

We all cracked up and headed to the backyard, where we danced, sang, and ate like crazy. Despite my heart still aching over Haneef, I'm sure that it was the best day of my life.

SPIN IT . . .

Track 27

It was sort of weird living back with my mother, especially living with her by myself. But true story, what was mad strange—but in a good way—was living with her being sober. Having a sober mom meant having someone who cared about where you went, what you did, and when you were coming home. Having a sober mother meant having someone who wanted to talk to you, truly get to know you, and I was definitely gonna ask her for money. She'd gotten a job at the hospital working in housekeeping.

She was sooooo proud of herself and I was, too. It was nice to see her become a new woman and I had to admit, it was even nicer having her to myself. Even if she got on my nerves about wanting to know my every move. But given what I'd been through, I could deal with that.

"Ma," I yelled from my room as I slid on my shoes. "I'm about to leave for work."

"Okay." She stood in my doorway and leaned against the frame. "What time will you be getting off?"

"About ten or eleven tonight."

"Okay, well call me first and I'll walk down there to meet you. I don't want you walking home alone."

"I'll be catching the bus, Ma." I placed my purse on my right shoulder.

"That's right," she said as she snapped her fingers. "Well then, call me when you get to the bus stop, and I'll come meet you—"

"Ma, I'll be okay."

"I know, but I just worry about you."

"Ma, you're being extra."

"Lee-Lee, I don't mean to be extra. Well . . ." she said, then paused, "I do mean to be extra. I just missed so much of your life, and for so long you were the mother around here and you never got to be the child—"

"Ma, you being sober is one of the greatest gifts you could give me. Now if you would excuse me, I need to go." I kissed her on the cheek. "Thank you."

"Oh, did I tell you the courts are going to let Ny'eem come home soon?"

"They dealt with his charges?"

"Yep, they had him complete a special program, which he did, and he should be back home with us sooner than you think."

"Yay!" I hugged her. "I miss him so much."

"I do, too. So, are you ready?" she asked me while grabbing her purse.

"Ready for what?"

"For work."

"What? You plan on going to work with me? Something I need to know about?" I asked with playful sarcasm in my tone.

"No smarty, but I am going to walk you to the bus stop."

"Okay, Ma," I sighed. Telling her not to come would be wasted breath. "Come on."

As we walked out of the building, my mother looked up and down the block. "I wish I could save enough money to get us out of here," she said as we started toward the bus stop. "This place is just the pits."

"It's okay, Ma. You're doing the best you can."

"I know, but I feel like I owe you so much."

"You need to stop worrying, please. You're doing the right thing. Did you go to your N.A. meeting this morning?"

"I sure did, and the group leader was fine, too."

"You are not supposed to be looking at men," I joked.

"I know and believe me, I'm not interested, not at this point in my recovery anyway. But I'm sayin', though, I'm not dead."

"Uhmm hmm, you're just fresh."

"Speaking of being fresh, what happened between you and Haneef?"

My heart jumped and the pain I'd been fighting

like hell to be rid of ached again. "Ma, I really don't wanna talk about that."

"Okay, Lee-Lee . . . well just tell me this. Do you think you'll ever forgive him?"

"Ma," I said as I shook my head and I felt tears sneaking up into my eyes. "I went through hell while I was with Haneef."

"It wasn't his fault though, Elite."

"No, not all of it. But it was just so much being with him, with the whole world in my business, and then Deidra."

"Who is Deidra?"

"His girlfriend."

"I thought you were his girlfriend. Was he cheating on you?"

"You know . . . sometimes I feel like maybe he wasn't, but then when I saw them on TV and he kissed her, I just couldn't take it anymore."

"Did you ask him about that?"

"Yeah."

"And what did he say?"

"I didn't give him a chance to explain."

"So, you really don't know what they were to each other."

"Ma, I can see. I have eyes and then he lied to me."

"Okay, maybe he shouldn't have lied. And he shouldn't have been kissing this Deidra chick either. But in that business, Elite, so much goes on, maybe it was publicity."

"Yeah, right." I twisted my lips as we stopped at

the bus stop and flagged the oncoming bus. "It wasn't publicity. He was just a liar."

After I boarded the bus and took my seat, I started to wonder if maybe it was publicity . . . and maybe . . . maybe I could forgive him. But, nah. I didn't even want to think about that. I had things just perfect, and the only problem I had was getting my heart to believe what my brain was telling me.

SPIN IT . . .

Track 28

"Lee-Lee," my mother called, waking me up out of my sleep. "Do you know someone named P-Twenty-Five . . . ?"

P-Twenty-Five? "No!"

"Oh, what's your name, baby?" I heard her say. "P-Thirty, no P-Fifty. What kinda name is that? I'm sure ya mama named you something decent."

P-Fifty? Was she talkin' to P-Fifty? What was he doing here? I snatched the phone off the receiver and called Naja. "Naja," I said as she answered the phone. "I think P-Fifty is here."

"I'm on my way!" she screamed and then hung up.

"Well, I'm sorry," I heard my mother say as I started throwing on clothes. "If you don't have another name besides P-Thirty-Five, you can't come in here to see my daughter."

I was praying for her to stop. "Ma," I said as I ran into the other room and saw P-Fifty standing there with Young Run, a new rapper who'd just come out. "Wait, I know him."

"You know him?" She looked at me like I was crazy. "Well, who the hell is he? And pull ya pants up." She frowned at Young Run. "And take off ya hat in my house."

"Ma, it's alright."

"Where they at?" Naja said as she flew in the door.

"Excuse me?" My mother looked at Naja as if she'd lost her mind.

"Young Run!" Naja said in a pant, grabbing his arm. "I'm Naja and I'm single." She looked at P-Fifty, "I can sing, too."

"Oh," I shook my head, slapping my hand over her mouth. "Please, please don't." I turned to P-Fifty. "We're just excited to see you here. Uhmmm, just never expected you would come over as a guest."

He smiled. "Listen, I won't be long. But Young Run here is a protégé of mine and you heard his hit single that's out right—"

Course Naja started dancing and singing, "It's official, I'm on a mission . . ." She started to rap, "Hollah, yeah, we heard of that. That's wassup, that joint is fiyah."

"All of this is just too much for me," my mother said. "I'm just gon' have a seat."

"Sorry to disturb you, ma'am," Young Run said.

"But check it," P-Fifty said to me. "We're about

to work on Young Run's new CD and after hearing you sing with Haneef, I couldn't get your face and your voice off my mind. So I wanted to offer you an opportunity to record with Young Run, as well as offer you a record deal."

"A who-who?"

"Say all that again," my mother said.

"Oh, my God," Naja started panting. "I always knew you had it in you. I always did. I would like to thank the Academy . . ."

I couldn't believe it. "You actually want me to sing on Young Run's CD, and you're willing to give me a record deal? A girl like me?"

"Why not? A girl like you could be the perfect one. And given all the stuff the papers said about you, hmph, you've got a story like a lot of other young girls. So who knows, maybe you'll be an inspiration to them."

I turned to my mother. "Ma, what do you think?"

"Depends on what you wanna do."

"I wanna do it!"

She looked at P-Fifty. "Seems like you got your answer!"

SPIN IT . . .

Track 29

I thought I was dreaming when I felt someone snatch the covers off me and the pillow from under my head. Then I opened my eyes and realized it was real, and Ny'eem was standing there. "Wake up!" I couldn't believe it. I started smiling and couldn't stop.

"I said get up."

I got up and hugged my brother so tightly that I fell on the bed with him and started planting sloppy kisses all over his face. "I can't believe you're home! Oh, I love you! I love you so much! Did you see Mommy? You see how pretty she is and how clean she is! Ny'eem, please don't get in trouble again, I couldn't take it with you being gone."

"Okay," he said in a scratchy voice. "Is that why you're trying to kill me?"

"Kill you?" I said, taken aback.

"I can't breathe, Elite."

"Oh." I loosened my grip. "My fault."

"Oh, no," floated from my doorway. "Y'all didn't start playing without us!"

When I looked up, I saw Aniyah, Sydney, and Mica. I ran and hugged them all of them at the same time.

"When did you get home?" I kept kissing them repeatedly.

"Mrs. Jameson dropped us off."

"Oh, my God. I missed you all so much."

"Mommy told us about your record deal."

"I sure did," my mother said as she walked in my room.

"Yo," Ny'eem said. "You think I could get a rap deal?"

"Yeah," Sydney said. "Especially now that you been to jail."

"Sydney!" my mother yelled. "Watch your mouth!"

"I was just playin'." She gave my mother a quick and appeasing smile.

"I bet you were." My mother started tickling her.

The entire scene was perfect and I didn't want anything to interrupt it. I was overjoyed beyond belief. I never imagined that my life would turn full circle like this. It was as if everything I'd been through was supposed to have happened so that it would add up to that very moment. That moment when we were together as a family, and no one could take us away from one another.

After a few hours of playing with my brothers and sisters, my mother called us into the kitchen for dinner.

"Ma, when you learn to cook?" Ny'eem asked her, surprised.

"Boy, hush," she laughed. "Your mama can burn."

"Exactly, that's what I'm sayin'. So when your food start tasting this good?"

"Funny."

I was laughing so hard tears were falling from my eyes. "Ma, Ny'eem is telling the truth. You know you use to mess up some food."

"I did not."

"Ma," I said and twisted my lips. "Be honest."

"Okay, maybe once in a while, but I'm better now. You have to admit this is the best fried chicken you've ever had."

"Fried chicken?!" we all said simultaneously. "We thought this was fish."

"Awwwl, man! We gon' order out from now on."

"I just need some practice," my mother said as if she were pleading for us to understand.

I fell out laughing until I cried. "Okay Ma, okay," I said, not wanting her feelings to be hurt. "Just forewarn us the next time."

"I got you forewarned."

After dinner we watched television, laughed,

and talked more. It was as if we were having a family reunion that none of us wanted to end.

"Let's play pitty-pat for pennies," Ny'eem suggested.

"Oh, you must wanna be spanked," I said, "'cause you know I got the juice when it comes to cards."

"Whatever, girl," Ny'eem said, grabbing the deck of cards as we all gathered back around the table. "Put up or shut up."

"I wanna play," Aniyah said.

"Me too!" Sydney chimed.

"And don't forget me," Mica insisted as he wrapped his favorite sheet around his neck. "I wanna play, too."

"Boy, if you don't get your Superman behind outta here!" Ny'eem snapped.

"Mommy!"

"Yes," she called from the kitchen as she washed the dishes.

"Ny'eem is teasing me."

"Cut it out, Ny'eem."

"I'm just playin', man," he said, motioning for Mica to sit next to him. "We the two men around here. We have to look out for each."

"That's what I'm talkin' about," Mica nodded. "Hey, Ny'eem."

"Wassup?"

"Aniyah said you knew how to make license plates. Is that true?"

"Ma!"

"Yes, Ny'eem!"

"Get these kids."

"Cut it out, kids."

I looked at my brothers and sisters, and couldn't stop smiling. The evening was beyond my wildest dreams.

SPECIAL REQUEST

(Love Letter)

"Wassup everybody?! This is DJ Twan from Hot 102, and I have with me the newest hip-hop female sensation, Elite. Wassup Elite?"

I had spent at least at hour telling myself I would be calm when it came to doing this promotion/radio interview, yet my heart skipped around in my chest cavity like crazy, so I prayed I spoke with ease: "Everything is everything, DJ Twan." I smiled and DJ Twan winked his eye at me. I could tell he knew I was nervous. I looked at Naja sitting in the corner of the studio, and she gave me a thumbs up.

"You know," I continued, "my CD, *A Girl Like Me*, dropped last week—"

"And it's killin' the charts!" DJ Twan said excitedly. "We gon' spin that new joint in a minute,

'Love Letter.' So Elite, is it true that you wrote that?"

"Yes," I blushed. "I wrote five tracks on my CD. As well as a couple of tracks for Chris Brown, Neyo, Dream, and for a new upcoming artist."

"Did you write 'Love Letter' for anybody in particular?"

"Maybe," I smiled.

"Ai'ight, Miss Maybe. Congrats on doing so well! Do your thang, girl! Well, we're here to promote your new CD, and to give away tickets to your upcoming concert at the Garden, with special guest stars Lil Wayne and Keyshia Cole! You must be amped about that!"

"Am I? What, don't play with me!"

DJ Twan laughed. "So, I tell you what, let's get to giving some of these tickets away. Call us up," he spoke into the microphone, "and to everybody out there listening, if you want tickets, then you need to call us and let us know why you love Elite so much that you should be front and center at the concert! But first, let's listen to this hot new joint. Elite—"

"Yes."

"Why don't you sing a few bars for your fans?"

"And you know this." I smiled as my "Love Letter" bed dropped. I started adlibbing, and then floated into singing the jam.

I closed my eyes and heard myself singing into the earphones. I thought about how much I'd been through and how I never imagined where my life would end up.

Here I was here on the radio, the very station where all of this started. And though I'd never been happier in my life, there was one problem: I missed Haneef.

I felt like he should've been there to share the moment with me. I felt incomplete, at times lost, and every day I felt lonely. And no matter how long we'd been apart, I wanted him back desperately. But obviously, since I hadn't heard from him in three months, he didn't feel the same way. I hoped as I sang my hit single, which I wrote for him—that if and when he ever took the time to listen to it, that he would realize it was our jam. I ended the tune and wiped the twinkle of a tear forming in the corner of my eye.

"Man, that was hot!" DJ Twan said when I stopped singing. "You got skills for real. You gon' be around a long time!"

"Thank you."

"Ai'ight, Ms. Elite, so let's get to giving these tickets away. The phone lines are lit up. And let's take caller . . . ten. Wassup caller? What's your name and where are you from?"

"Oh, my God!" a girl screamed. "Elite, you remember me?! It's Ciera! From school. Wassup girl?"

I couldn't believe it! "I just wanted you to know that I am your biggest fan, and I always knew you would make it!"

Oh . . . kay . . . "Hi, Ciera. Thanks for the encouragement."

"So can I get those tickets?"

Was this chick asking me for tickets? When she had dogged me in school? When she and Jahaad were the ones who posted that article telling the whole world that my mother was on drugs. This chick had major nerve. I didn't want to think about my reputation, so I could tell this chick to step her ass off and be gone. But . . . my manager and record company would have a fit, so I didn't. Instead I said, "No, Ciera, I don't quite remember you, but anyway gurl, tell me why you should get these tickets."

"You don't remember me?! Oh, you done got all famous and crazy!" Ciera started going off. "I know you don't think—"

"Okay," DJ Twan clicked her off the line. "Next caller."

I couldn't believe Ciera. All I could do was look at Naja, who laughed so loud the engineer had to ask her to be quiet. In the midst of laughing at Ciera, DJ Twan took a few more callers and gave away two sets of tickets.

"Ai'ight, down to our last pair. Three times a charm! The hotline is lit up like crazy, so caller, tell us why you love Elite!"

"Because the first time I saw her," a familiar male voice said, "I knew it was love. And you know I had her once and I lost her."

My heart jumped. For a moment I thought the

caller was Haneef, but nah, I knew it wasn't . . . Naja looked at me strangely; apparently she thought
 the same thing. "How'd you lose her?" I asked.

"Because I did something stupid for publicity. I listened to my publicist tell me that I needed to be with some girl just for show, and didn't think about how I would hurt the girl I loved. So I did it and now I'm here, trying to confess my love."

I couldn't believe it. It was Haneef. Tears were racing like a marathon from my eyes.

"And I love you for so many different reasons, Li'l Ma. I love the way your dimples light up when you laugh. The way you hold your hands and bite your bottom lip when you're nervous." DJ Twan looked at me and mouthed, "You know who this is?"

I shook my head yes.

DJ Twan spoke into the microphone: "Can I ask your name, caller?"

"Haneef."

"*The* Haneef?" DJ Twan looked surprised, and so did everyone else in the room. "*The Haneef,* like platinum selling *Haneef*?"

"Exactly, and I want the world to know that I love Elite. She's my heart, my world, my wifey, and I can't stand being without her any longer . . ."

The more he spoke, the closer he felt and the louder his voice sounded to me. I held my head down. I hated that I was crying like this, especially since I wasn't one who wore my feelings on my fingertips. And just as I wiped my eyes and decided that after I left here, I was pushing all my stupid anger to the side and going to get my boo, I felt my chair spin around. I opened my eyes and Haneef was squatting before me.

"I can't do it anymore." He placed his cell phone on the table. "I need you and I love you too much to be without you."

"I guess this means you don't really want the tickets, huh?" DJ Twan laughed.

"Nah," Haneef smiled. "I don't want any tickets. I just want you, Elite."

"You better stop crying," Naja whispered as she tapped me on the shoulder, "and get with this cat before I do."

Only Naja.

I sniffed and got myself together. No more being without him. No more being stubborn. None of that mattered. All that mattered was that I was Haneef's girl. I took off the headphones, stood up, and embraced my baby tightly.

"I want you to be my girl." He looked at me, wiping my tears away.

"Yes." I kissed him. "Yes, I'll be your girl."

And as if on cue, they dropped a recording of the duet we did at his concert that night I first got onstage with him.

Haneef and I held each other tightly as we kissed passionately, and I knew at that moment I would never let him go. He took the chain he wore around his neck, the one that he'd given me before, and placed it back on me.

"I love you, Elite," he whispered to me.

"And I love you, too."

SPIN TO DA END

My mother sat the old boom box we used to jam to on the kitchen windowsill. Then she popped in my new CD and placed it on mixed rotation while Ny'eem rapped and Mica, Sydney, and Aniyah danced. The movers were buzzing and placing furniture all around us and though everyone else seemed to be happy we were moving to Westchester, New York—a place where there was more than an inground pool waiting in the backyard, there was a brand new start and a chance to be anything we wanted to be—I had to admit I was scared.

It was like . . . really stepping out there, really having to rely on ourselves and depending on no one else but each other. Which all added up to the fact that there was a lot riding on my mother's sobriety.

And I wasn't exactly sure how to do it, but I knew I had to trust her. And I had to step back enough for her to be exactly who she was . . . a mother . . . my mother . . . our mother.

And that was when I realized that all the time I'd been holding my breath, maybe . . . just maybe . . . it was the moment to release it. No more hiding, no more lying, or being embarrassed of who I was.

After all, Cassie was completely different. She was no longer hanging out in the streets or yelling at us through a crack in the bathroom door while she got high. She attended N.A. faithfully, went to church religiously, and most of all was a mom—a regular mom—who not only loved us but cooked for us, ironed for us, washed our clothes, and spent time with us.

As everyone continued about their business preparing for the move, I tipped into my old room and looked around. I lay down on the bed and stared at the ceiling. All I could do was smile, because never in a million years had I imagined this life.

"Yo, Li'l Ma. You ready to roll?" Haneef stood in my doorway. He looked around my room, amazed. "When did you do all of this?" He glared at the pink painted walls, the brand new white poster bed, and everything else that made the room fit for a princess.

"Last night."

"Why?"

"I wanted to make the little girl moving in here feel as if she had a chance."

"That's real sweet, baby."

"Actually, I ordered furniture for the whole place."

"Wow, look at you. Let me find out—you tryna be Robin Hood and er'thing."

"Be quiet." I laughed.

"Nah, Li'l Ma, this is real nice, though." Haneef walked over to the bed and lay down next to me. "But . . . ahhh . . . why are we laying here?" He kissed me.

"Cause I'm trying to remember when it all happened, and when life started to really change, and I can't quite think of it. All I know is that somehow, I'm here."

"That's how it is, Li'l Ma. One day you look up and go dang, God, you the man."

I looked at my boo and my whole face lit up. That was exactly it. Exactly! It all started with me talking to God. And it was the perfect way to end it, too, by saying, "Dang, God, You are the man!"

"Elite!" my mother called out to me. "Erika, Jena, and the boys are here."

"Who are they?" Haneef asked.

"The family who's moving in here. So you better get up." I looked at Haneef and pushed him on the shoulder. "Especially if you don't want Cassie to wreck shop on you."

He laughed. "I sure don't."

"Elite!" Erika ran into my room, followed by my mother, and Erika's mother, Jena.

"My goodness!" Jena exclaimed.

"Elite," Erika said in awe. "This room is for a princess!"

"And that's exactly what you are." I hugged her.

Jena was in tears and I could hear the boys screaming about how great their rooms were.

"I can't believe you did all of this for us," Jena cried. "Thank you so much!"

Erika continued to hug me tightly and screamed, "Thank you! I can't believe all of this is for me!" She looked at Haneef and just when I thought her screams couldn't get any louder, they soared through the roof. "Oh, my God, my friend said you were best friends with Rekeem! I mean I love your music and everything, but er'body knows that Elite has you on lock!"

I laughed and bumped Haneef on the shoulder. "On lock, huh?"

"Don't sweat yourself," he mumbled.

"But do you know Rakeem?!" Erika screamed.

"Yes," Haneef said.

"Oh . . . my . . . God! Tell him I love him. As a matter of fact, my mom said I could call the radio station to win tickets to his concert! It's next week and I just have to be there! And all I have to do is sing." She held up a poster she had in hand. "And I'll have you know I can sing. Trust me, one day

I'ma be just like Elite! Now," she spun on her heels, "where should I put this?"

I smiled at my mother and then Haneef. "Okay," I said, pulling out a roll of tape. "Put this," I said as I stood in the center of her bed and she handed me her Rakeem poster, "right here." And I taped it to her ceiling.

She lay down on the bed and looked at the ceiling. "Ahhhh, now this is what I call the life."

A READING GROUP GUIDE

A GIRL LIKE ME

Ni-Ni Simone

ABOUT THIS GUIDE

The following questions are intended to enhance your group's reading of A GIRL LIKE ME.

Discussion Questions

1. What did you think of Elite running the household in the beginning of the story? Do you think it was realistic? Why or why not? Do you think there are teenagers who take care of their siblings the same or similar ways?

2. What did you think about Elite and Naja "borrowing" the clothes from their job? Do you think it was stealing? Would you have done the same thing? Why or why not?

3. Did you think that Elite was easily influenced by Naja, especially when it came to doing the wrong things? Have you ever been influenced by someone in the same way?

4. Do you think Jahaad loved Elite? Why or why not?

5. Do you think Haneef loved Elite? Why or why not?

6. Have you ever dreamed of dating a superstar? If so, do you think you would have gone through some of the things Elite and Haneef went through?

7. Do you think Elite should have lied about her "real" life to Haneef? Why or why not?

8. Do you think Haneef was right when he took Deidra to the awards? Why or why not?

9. Do you think that Elite should have taken Haneef back?

10. What do you think Elite's life will be like now that she's famous?

A Discussion with the Author

What do you like most about being an author?

What I like most is that I can bring all of my dreams to life. If I want to be a singer, a dancer, or a rapper, then I can be. The world on paper is limitless. But I couldn't do it without my education. And no, I'm not a walking afterschool special, but I do keep it real. I know I couldn't write books without paying attention in my English classes, and when it came to the literary contracts, math was useful, too—LOL.

What is one of the best things you've ever done?

Uhmmm, okay, dump a boy who didn't treat me like a lady. I had to let him know he had me twisted.

Name one of the worst things you've ever done?

Date a boy I didn't like.

Who is your favorite rapper?

You know it's Bow Wow.

Who is your favorite famous couple?

Beyoncé and Jay-Z. They are so hot!

What's your favorite TV show?

Actually, I have two: *Run's House* and Keyshia Cole's reality show, *The Way It Is*. Oh, and *Flavor of Love.* Wait, wait, oh yeah, BET's *Hell Date*. *I Love New York* is the bomb, too. And I do have two oldies but goodies, *Good Times* and *Little House on the Prairie*. What, chile please, can you say J.J. and Nellie Oleson? I know that was more than two.

What lesson do you want readers to learn from *Shortie Like Mine*?

To never doubt yourself, and to know that the sky is the limit.

Want more?
Check out SHORTIE LIKE MINE and
IF I WAS YOUR GIRL
by Ni-Ni Simone.
Available now wherever books are sold.

Shortie Like Mine

1

I ain't even gonna front . . .
Since you walked up in the club
I've been giving you the eye . . .
Must be a full moon . . .

—BRANDY, "FULL MOON"

It was official: I was fly. I had on my freakum dress and the fat version of Lil Wayne was stalking me. Everywhere I looked, there he was. Grinning. As if somebody here in Newark, New Jersey, told him he was cute. He had drips of sweat running from his temples to his chin and was breathing like he was having an asthma attack. I was embarrassed. Out of all the tenders lined up outside the club, hugged up on their honeys, and kicking it with their boys, here I was being harassed by a baby gorilla in a short set.

My girls and I were in line, waiting to get in to Club Arena for teen night, and for the first time in my life, I was appreciating my size fourteen brickhouse hips. My hair was done in a cute ponytail, swinging to the side with a swoop bang in the front, my MAC was poppin', and my stilettos were workin' it out.

I resembled a voluptuous New New from *ATL*: two deep dimples, honey glazed skin, full lips, and dark brown eyes shaped like a lost reindeer. My sleeveless House of Dereon dress was the color of new money and the belt wrapped around my waist was metallic silver. My colorful bangles and big hoop earrings were courtesy of Claire's and the rose tattoo on my left calf was by way of the 99 Cent Store and warm water. So, you get the picture? Fierce was written all over me. And just when I started feeling comfortable with being the biggest one in my all-girl clique, tragedy struck. . . .

"Yo, Shawtie!" my stalker screamed as if he were working at the Waffle House, making a public service announcement. He was standing at the door talking to one of the bouncers, when my friend Deeyah walked up and stood beside me. "Yo, Shawtie," he called again. "Deeyah"—he raised his arm in the air as if he were making a three-point play—"that's me right there."

My girls and I all looked around. We ain't know who the *heck* he was talking about.

"Seven, there go your new boo." Deeyah blew a pink bubble and popped it. "The one and only Melvin. Told you I was gon' hook you up."

Melvin? I tugged Deeyah on her arm. "Is this a joke?"

"What's wrong with him?" she snapped, rolling her eyes. "You tryna talk about my taste?"

Oh . . . my . . . God . . . I'ma die. "He looks like my sixty-year-old Cousin Shake."

"Everything is not about looks, Seven. When are you gon' to grow up and learn that?"

"When I'm done with being sixteen, which is not today. I don't believe this."

"Well, who did you think you were gon' get?" She popped her gum and smiled. "After all, Josiah is mine and the rest of his crew, well . . . I hooked them up," she said as she pointed at each of our friends: Ki-Ki, Yaanah, and Shae.

Ki-Ki and Yaanah shot me a snide grin as if to say, *That's right!* But Shae rolled her eyes and said, "Please, Deeyah. You lucky I ain't punch you in the face for that. Gon' hook me up with somebody named Shamu."

"Shamu is a nice name." Deeyah jerked her neck.

"But he followed me around in school." Shae sighed. "From class to class, and then I come to find out he was the oldest kid in special ed."

"Special ed?" Deeyah pointed to her chest. "He's in my class. So what you tryna say, Shae? So what if he wears a helmet? He needs love, too."

A helmet?

"Why"—Shae looked toward the sky—"do I even go through this?"

"Go through what?" Deeyah smirked. "Why don't you think about the future, Shae? Don't you know people in special ed get a check every month? Never mind, Shae. You just played yourself." She turned her attention back to me. "Seven, I know you got more sense than this chick, so you know you need a man that you gon' complement. Trust me. See, Josiah needs a chick like me. I'm a dime and you're a quarter. Josiah is the captain of the basketball team and Melvin over there"—she pointed—"is the team. Make sense?"

We all looked at Deeyah like she was stupid. "Can you say dumb-dumb?" I shook my head. "You so busy tryna dis me that you actually just gave me and ole boy over there a compliment."

"Girl, please. That flew over your head," Deeyah snapped. "You just played yourself."

"Deeyah, you just said you were a dime and she was a quarter." Shae sighed. "Get a clue."

"I could get a clue if I could stop passing it to you." Deeyah rolled her eyes. "Y'all so stupid. I'm tired of being the mother of this played-out group. Anyway, Seven, I called myself doing you a favor."

"A favor?"

"Yeah, I'm tryna save you from being played."

"Excuse you?!" I could've smacked her.

"Think of it this way. If a guy is too fly, he might leave you for a skinny chick." She ran her hands along the sides of her body. "And with Rick Ross over there"—she snickered—"you ain't got to worry 'bout that."

Before I could decide if I wanted to body her or simply cuss her out, I felt a tap on my shoulder and hot breath on my neck. "What's good, Shawtie?" It was Melvin, looking me up and down as if he could take a biscuit and sop me up with his eyes. "I knew I'd seen you before—good look, Deeyah."

"You've seen me?" *I don't think I've been to hell yet.*

"Yeah, I pass you every day on my way to English class."

"Really?" I was beyond disgusted.

"Come on, Shawtie, ain't you in them honors classes? You real smart and er'thang." He had the biggest grin I'd ever seen. "My pot'nahs call me Big Country. But my name is Melvin. I just moved here from Murfreesboro."

"Murphy who?"

"Carolina, Shawtie." His gold tooth was gleaming. "You know, I-95 in the house, the dirty-dirty baby."

I was speechless. Not only was he fat, he was country.

"Speechless, huh? You ain't never seen nobody reppin' for the dirty-dirty like me befo'." As if he had a bullhorn and was doing the lean-back, he cupped each hand on the sides of his mouth and shouted, "MUR . . . FREES . . . BORO!!!"

God must hate me.

"I know you feelin' me, Shawtie." He grabbed me by the arm and pulled me toward him. "Gurl, you so sharp, you hurtin' me. Now, let's get on in here. You ain't got to wait in no line. We just gon' walk on in this piece. Now ya gurls, I can't do nothin' for them. Big Country's pull is limited."

"Oh, it's okay." I shook my head. "Really, it is. I'll just wait with them. You go on."

“Sab, Shawtie.” He pinched my cheek. “I was just playin’. Psyched yo’ mind.” He ran his index finger across my forehead. “Y’all get on here and come on in this piece. Deeyah and Shawtie, y’all hold arms and y’all other two walk in front of me and let them know Big Country has arrived.”

“That’s all you, Melvin?” someone shouted as we walked in.

“All day playboy,” he shouted back. “All day.”

Jesus please . . .

As soon as we walked in, the bass in the music sent vibrations through the floor. The D.J. was doing his thang—Baby Huey’s “Pop, Lock, and Drop It” was playing and instantly, everyone, including Melvin, started dancing. I stood leaning from one foot to the other, wondering what punishment I faced next.

And just when I decided I should find a rock to climb under, Melvin threw his hands in the air and screamed, “This my jam right here!!” “Walk It Out” started playing and Melvin took to the floor again.

After the song finished, Melvin bought me a drink and dragged me to take a few Polaroids with him. In the midst of him squattin’, leanin’, and showcasin’ a few jailhouse poses with me standing completely still, Josiah, Deeyah’s boyfriend and number twenty-three on the school’s basketball team, swaggered over with an entourage of his teammates. Two things about Josiah and his crew was that they were the finest in school and all the girls wanted them. But me, I only had eyes for Josiah and when I found out Deeyah was dating him, I think I passed out every day for a week straight. She must've stolen him out of my dreams because that's the only way I could see me allowing her to walk away with him. Other than that, we woulda been throwin'. Please believe dat. But since I didn't think I had a real chance of him liking me, I stepped to the side and have been diggin' him from afar.

Josiah had a super-sized Uptown in his hand. He shook the ice, handed the cup to Deeyah, and she finished it off. Then he stood behind her with his fingers locked around her waist, his chin on top of her head, and he started staring at me.

Chris Brown's "Shortie Like Mine" was playing and for a moment I could swear Josiah's eyes were singing the lyrics to me. This made me want him even more. The crush I had on him was unshakable. He was not only the most wanted man in school, he was the best looking. He was so beautiful I was tempted to call him pretty. He superseded fine, and gorgeous couldn't touch him. He was the type of dude who should've been a poster child for irresistible. Most people said he favored the rapper Nelly, but personally, I thought he put Nelly to sleep. He was so fine, it didn't make sense. He was at least six feet, with skin the color of caramel in its richest form, the sexiest almond-shaped eyes in the world, and a fresh Caesar with brushed-in waves. His gear was always dapper: baggy jeans, an oversize skull belt buckle, a fitted black tee that read "I am Hip Hop," and throwback Pumas.

"Can't speak, Seven?" he asked.

I know he had to hear my heart beating. "No," I snapped, and as an extra twist, I rolled my eyes.

"Yo, Josiah," Melvin interrupted. "Back up off me now. You know this is me right here."

"Yo, my fault, son." He smiled. "Do you."

"Whew, Shawtie," Melvin said, dapping sweat like a church lady in heat. "Give ya boo a sip of that soda."

Oh, he had me messed up. There was no way we'd reached the level of drinking after one another. "You see the bar over there." I pointed. "Go fetch yo'self one."

"Fetch?" Josiah snapped. "He ain't a dog."

"Is that why you responded?" I asked.

"You tryna say I'ma dog?"

"I'm tryna say you all up in here wit' it." I waived my hand under my chin as if I were slicing it.

"Dang, Shawtie, you just angry, huh?" Melvin said. "What, you P.M.S.'n or somethin'? Somebody hook my girl up with some Midol."

His girl?

"Now, Shawtie," Melvin went on, "act right in front of company and gimme some of that soda." He snatched the cup from my hand and I snatched it back, causing it to spill and splatter all over my dress.

"What, are you *stupid?!*" I couldn't believe this. "Oh, my God, you ruined my dress! You just dumb! Who invented you? Dang, you . . . get . . . on . . . my . . . nerves! Why don't you take I-95 and ride you and yo' gold tooth back down south. Uggggg! What crime did I commit to get hooked up with you?!" I hated being so mean, but didn't he ask for it? Looking at Melvin, I could tell I hurt his feelings because for the first time tonight he was silent.

"Yo," Josiah snapped, releasing his hands from around Deeyah's waist and standing up straight. "I think you owe my man an apology."

"Apology? If anything, you need to apologize for being up in my business!" I shouted. "Ain't nobody talkin' to you!"

"You know what?" Josiah said with extreme bass in his voice. "You gotta nasty attitude. And I really don't know what it's for, 'cause you look ridiculous, rockin' a buncha knockoff. If you so miserable, why don't you take ya fat ass home!"

Every tear I had in my body filled my mouth, which is why I couldn't speak. Yaanah and Ki-Ki were looking around the club as if they hadn't heard anything. When I looked at Deeyah, she'd covered her lips with her right hand and a snide smile was sneaking out the side. Shae was standing there in disbelief, looking at Josiah as if at any moment she was about to give it to him. "You know I got yo' back," she said.

I wanted to cry so badly, but I'd been played out enough and if I let this slide, then all of them standing there would think they had the upper hand. So, this is what I did—I blacked on all of 'em. Straight up, I was 'bout to read 'em. "Deeyah, Yaanah, and Ki-Ki, I know y'all ain't laughin'." I looked at Shae for confirmation. "Should I get 'em, gurl?"

"Get 'em, gurl, 'cause I'ma get ole boy over here when you done." She placed her hand on her right hip and looked toward Josiah.

I snapped my neck. "Let me set you on fire real quick. We 'spose to be homegirls and y'all standin' here laughin', when everybody here know you three are the queens of knockoff. If it wasn't for y'all, the Ten-Dollar Store woulda been closed down! You Payless-Target-Wal-Mart-havin' Salvation Army freaks. Look like you get ya clothes out the Red Cross box. And word is, Josiah, you buy all of Deeyah's gear, so what that make you?"

"A hot-ass mess." Shae rolled her eyes in delight. "Looks like you been shut down, Superman."

"Whew, look at you girl," Melvin said, looking at Shae. "I likes me some aggressive women. Maybe I oughta hollah you. What's your name?"

"Boy, please," Shae said.

Josiah shot me a snide smile. "Your mouth is ridiculous." He eyed Deeyah and the expression on his face seemed to dance in laughter. "Y'all shot out."

"I don't believe you went there, Seven," Deeyah said. "You know Ki-Ki ain't boostin' from the Red Cross box no more."

"Don't be tryna call me out!" Ki-Ki shouted. "That was Yaanah's idea anyway."

"Oh, no, you didn't . . . !"

And the next thing I knew, these three were in a brawl over whose idea it was to jack the donation-clothing bin. But hmph, I didn't care. What difference did it make to me when I felt like the whole club was still trippin' off how bad Josiah played me. I knew it was time for me to roll, I just didn't want it to seem like I was running from something, or better yet, someone. "I'm not beat for this." I managed to keep the tears that flooded my mouth at bay. I turned to Melvin. "My fault if I hurt your feelings."

"Oh, you ain't hurt my feelings, Shawtie. That just turned me on."

If I didn't feel like crying, I would've laughed. "I'm 'bout to bounce."

"Hold up, Seven," Shae called from behind me. " 'Cause I'm 'bout to bounce with you."

And just like *America's Next Top Model,* we threw our right shoulders forward, our bootylicious oceans in motion, and proceeded out the door.

If I Was Your Girl

1

"This is my jam, right here!" I screamed as we drove down Bergen Street with the sounds of Playaz Circle's "Duffle Bag Boy" blasting from the car into the street. We'd just left the Hot 97 King of Rap concert at the Prudential Center and were still high from the night's festivities.

"Girl, did you see how Lil Wayne was looking at me?" my sister, Seven, said as she danced in the backseat.

"You lying, Seven," Tay laughed, as she drove down the street, looking at her in the rearview mirror. "You know Weezie was lookin' at me."

"I know y'all ain't on my baby daddy!" I stopped singing long enough to chime in.

"Girl, please," Seven snapped. "You got enough baby daddies!"

We all laughed as I turned up the volume and

started singing again. *"I ain't nevah ran from a damn thing and I damn sure ain't 'bout to pick today to start runnin'."*

As I threw my arms in the air, Tay said, "Toi, ain't that Quamir's truck?" She pointed across Rector Street.

I looked at the tags on the black Escalade. "Hell, yeah." I turned the music down.

"And ain't that Shanice's house?" Seven asked. "I thought he stopped messing with her."

"We don't know if that's her house," I snapped defensively. "You always jumping to conclusions."

Tay looked at me out the corner of her eyes. "You need to stop frontin'," she spat, "you know that's where the skeezer lives." Tay double parked in the street, next to Quamir's truck. "Now the question is, what you gon' do about it?"

"Nothin'," Seven jumped in. "You don't bring it to nobody else's spot." She sucked her teeth. "If anything we can slice his tires and bounce."

"Slice his tires?" Tay snapped. "That is so whack." She looked at me. "You know this is ridiculous, right? And I'm not slicing no tires or breaking no windows, he gon' put up or shut up. 'Cause frankly, I can't take you crying over this dude anymore."

"Confront him and what?" Seven spat. "If we not gon' key up his ride then we need to bounce." She turned to me. "You've seen it with your own eyes, so now you know you need to leave 'im alone." Seven wiggled her neck from side to side.

"Bounce?" Tay sucked her teeth. "Girl, please, we 'bout to handle this."

Neither of them had noticed that I hadn't said a word. I was in shock, but then again I wasn't. I just wasn't in the mood to react to something that obviously wasn't going to change, but there was no way I could let my sister or my best friend think I was gon' allow Quamir to keep playing me. I had to stand up for something, so I twisted my neck and rolled my eyes. "I'ma ring the trick's bell."

"There it is," Tay said. "There it is, and you know I got your back."

At least for pride's sake I had to pretend like I was strong. Strong enough, to at least beat this bitch's ass for being with my baby daddy. "I'm 'bout to wild-out!"

"This what you do," Tay said as we got out the car. "When she comes to the door, drag her ass down the stairs. Don't even show her no mercy. She knew Quamir was your dude, yet she keeps calling him over here. Nah, we gon' end this right now." Tay's lips popped twice as she zigzagged her neck. She was the spitting image of the ghetto twins in *ATL*, with the attitude to match, which is why I knew that if nothing else I could always count on her to be down with the get down. Even when I just wanted to curl up and die, she was on guard.

"You know this don't make no sense, right?" Seven said as she got out the car. "Mommy will kick *our* asses if she knew we were out here like this! Forget Quamir!"

"Forget Quamir? Do you know how bad he keep doggin' this fool?" Tay pointed at me.

"Don't call me no fool." I rolled my eyes as we walked up the steps.

"My fault." She gave me a crooked smile. "You know what I mean. Anyway, Seven, do you know this is like . . . the nineteenth time we ready to pounce on ole boy? Girl, please forget Quamir. He's takin' time away from me and my man. I wish I would—"

"Tay." I was pissed and she was making it worse. "You don't even have a man."

"Exactly," she whispered as I rang the bell. "And I'm not gon' get one chasing behind yours."

"Excuse you?" I sucked my teeth.

"Don't get mad, kick ass. Show 'em what's really hood. I'm tired of this dude playing you every other week. Shit, I need some sleep."

"This don't make no sense." Seven tapped her foot standing behind me. I could feel the warmth of her breath as she sighed against my neck.

"For real, y'all," I said. "Not now, 'cause the way I feel, y'all 'bout to get it. So my suggestion to you," I looked at Seven and then at Tay, "is to fall back."

"Excuse you?" Seven blinked her eyes.

"Be clear," Tay spat. "T-skee ain't the one. Let Quamir and his new skeezer be the only ones you feel comfortable bringin' it to—"

"No, I don't appreciate—"

"Toi—" Tay interrupted me.

"Don't cut me off!"

"Would you shut up?" she said, tight-lipped with arched eyebrows. "Somebody's comin' to the door!"

Immediately, all the air left my body as I watched Quamir open the door with Shanice standing beside him. I couldn't believe this was happening to me, especially since I knew Shanice. I mean, we weren't friends, but we went to school together and she knew Quamir was my man.

I could feel my eyes knocking in the back of my head, but now was not the time to cry. So I held my tears back as best I could, and looked at Shanice's face. I couldn't deny how pretty she was, and for a moment I wondered if Quamir thought she was prettier than me. We were both the color of fresh apple butter, yet her eyes glistened like full moons, while mine were almond shaped. I had a dimpled smile and she had a wide one. Unless I had my hair flat-ironed straight, it fell over my shoulders in an abundance of ocean waves, but ole girl wore a cheap blond clip weave. Wait a minute, I just found a flaw, at least my hair is real. Now I had the souped-up confidence I needed to handle my business. "This what you want, Quamir?"

"Yo," he said, surprised. "What are you doing here?"

"What you think?" I pointed my hand like a gun in his face, yet looking dead in hers. "This the tramp you want?"

"What is she doin' at my door, Quamir? You don't be coming to my house!" Shanice screamed, jumping up and down, acting as if at any moment she was gon' bring it.

"I know she ain't stuntin'," Tay snapped. "Oh, hell no!"

"And what?" Shanice hunched her shoulders. "He don't want her and she knows it!"

True story, I wanted to just walk away, but my mixed emotions wouldn't let me leave like that. I needed Quamir to see the pain on my face, and then maybe he would understand what he was doing to me. I felt like I was in a trance, or better yet blazed; like everything was moving in slow motion, a euphoric high that made me feel like nothing was real. Nevertheless, I had to do this. I had to teach this chick a lesson about messing with my man or better yet, teach him a lesson about messing around on me.

Therefore, I pushed all rational thought out of my mind and let my heart and bruised emotions lead the way. I reached over Quamir's shoulder and yanked Shanice by the hair. All hell broke loose! I pounced on my prey like crazy, sending the entire porch into an uproar. I'm not sure how Quamir moved out of the way, but all I knew is that he was standing there watching as I dragged her down the stairs by her hair, causing parts of her weave to fly into the breeze.

"What I tell you about my man, trick!" I swung with all I had as I pulled her into the street. The flashing streetlamp that shone above us splashed like a spotlight into her frightened face.

"Toi!" Quamir screamed, running down the stairs, the soles of his Timberlands thumping against the wood. "Yo, chill."

Chill? To hell with chill—all chill could do for me at that moment was get its ass beat.

"What?" Tay said in killer mode. "I know you ain't tryna do nothin', Quamir!"

Quamir ignored her. Instead, he stood there watching with his left thumb tucked behind his belt buckle with a smirk on his face, all while I beat this girl down.

The girl threw a punch, but I ducked, came back up, and caught her in the chin.

"Shanice, Toi, I said chill," Quamir said with ease. I could tell he wanted to laugh because I could hear the sounds in his throat.

Although Shanice was trying to fight back, I was beatin' on her like crazy as Quamir stood there and watched as if this was his favorite pastime entertainment.

"Slap her!" Tay shouted. "Her face is clear again, Toi!"

"That's enough!" Seven yelled as she tried to pull me off of Shanice. Seeing that she wasn't successful, Quamir jumped in and lifted me up by my waist. Instantly, the fight ceased.

As Quamir put me down, he stood with his back to me as Shanice ran up and started pushing her chest against his. "Get out the way!"

My chest was heaving up and down. "Bring it!" I spat. "Bring . . . it!"

Tay shot me a high five, and wagged her tongue out like a salivating dog. "You . . . spank dat . . . ass!" She hunched her shoulders toward Shanice, who was still pushing against Quamir. "Booyah!"

"Yo," Quamir pushed Shanice back. "What I say?"

"Bring it! Please bring it!" I was screaming at the top of my lungs.

"Let me go, Quamir!" Shanice pushed against him and pointed at me. "I promise you, I'ma get you jumped, you ain't gon' never be able to walk these streets again! You really don't know who I am!"

"You ain't shit!" I yelled. "I just whooped yo' ass in front of your house and ain't nobody come out to help you? Girl, please."

"My mother ain't home, otherwise she'd would've shot yo' azz!"

I yawned, and tapped my lips, "What . . . eva!"

Shanice snorted, her weave hanging by a strand on her head. "You crazy bitch!" She struggled to reach for me. "I hate you! You know I'ma kill her, Quamir!"

"Chill," he said sternly.

"This yo' chick, Quamir?" I mushed him in the back of his head. "This your girl?"

"I'm his baby's mother, you stupid jump-off! He told you to step but you keep holding on!"

Did she just say baby mother? I looked at Tay for confirmation and her face went from confident and proud to surprised. Then I looked at Seven, who wore an "*I told you so*" face.

Whatever. How she gon' have a baby by him and I just had one? This chick lyin'. "He ain't never told me to step," I carried on. "You wish! And girl, you don't have no baby by him. Please!" *Of all things, I know Quamir wouldn't have no baby on me. We were a family; his other two baby mamas were crazy, I wasn't, which is why he told me I was the one.* I looked at Shanice, "Lose ya'self!"

"Oh, you ain't never told her about our son, Quamir?" Shanice said.

Son? I had the son.

"You ain't never told her to step, Quamir?" Shanice mushed Quamir in the face. "Oh, you her man?"

"What, you ain't know?" My words floated over his shoulder. "You better tell her somethin', Quamir."

"Quamir!" Shanice screamed.

"Quamir," I shouted. "Tell her, and tell her to stop lying on you!"

Quamir's head turned back and forth from me to Shanice over and over again. For a moment, he looked as if he were going crazy, but I didn't care. I desperately wanted him to validate what I was saying and straight out call this girl a liar.

"Quamir!" Shanice and I screamed simultaneously.

"Yo, for real," he snapped. "Both y'all gettin'

on my nerves! True story, I ain't rockin' wit' neither one of y'all like that."

For some reason, as if we were doing a dance, we all stepped back. "What you say?" I think I heard wrong.

"Oh, you ain't with me, Quamir?" Shanice spat. "You been at my house every night this week and we ain't together? You're the one who asked me to have our baby so we would be a family—"

What she just say?

"And now," she continued on, "all of a sudden you ain't with me?" She pushed him in his chest. "Oh, we ain't together?"

He asked her what . . . ?

"Go 'head, Shanice." He pointed his finger in her face.

My voice trembled as I said, "I can't believe this!" I felt sooooo dumb. Here I was, battling with a buncha lies, fighting for the sake of proving a useless point.

"It's over, Quamir. This who you choosing?" I pointed over his shoulder. "You can have that stank ho! We through! You ain't nothin'; you don't take care of your son no way. Mama's boy! Trying so hard to be a playa but can't get outcha mama's basement. Your whole existence is a joke. I don't know whether to laugh in your face or spit in it."

I turned around to walk away, and Quamir yanked me by my hair so hard that I was dizzy. Seven and Tay immediately jumped between us. I looked at the rage in Quamir's eyes and I knew he wasn't playing. My heart thumped in my chest. "It's cool," I said to them as they stood in front of me.

"I been waitin' to kick yo' azz!" Tay said.

"Tay!" I snapped. "Chill. Y'all move and let me hear what he got to say." Before they could move on their own, Quamir pushed them to the side and stood in front of me.

"Who you talkin' to, Toi?" he said, sounding more like my father than my man.

I didn't answer.

"Don't you ever in your stupid life talk to me like that! You so stupid and dumb. This why don't nobody else want you! And no matter how I keep tryna stay with you, you keep actin' dumb! You need to get outta my business, retarded ho! You came around here actin' like a clown and all we gon' do is laugh at you."

"Don't be talking to her like that!" Seven screamed.

"You the stupid one!" Tay said.

"I know you ain't talkin' to me, you crazy ass, crack-head baby!" he spat with a sinister laugh.

"And what are you, Quamir?" Seven said. "At least Tay got an excuse."

Tay blinked her eyes. "Excuse me?"

"Ho, please," Quamir snorted. "I'm definitely not gon' argue with no virgin."

Feeling as if I was due to pass out at any minute, I fought with all I had to at least sound strong. "Boy, please. You been with this raggedy ho all week, and you talkin'!" The tears dancing in my throat stopped me mid-sentence. "This really yo' baby mama, Quamir?"

"Did I tell you I had another baby? Uh, answer me!"

Silence.

"Answer me!" he screamed.

"No!"

"Well then, why you assuming things?"

"What?" Shanice screamed, a flood of tears streaming down her face. "So what is you sayin'? That we don't have a son?" She punched him in his chest. "You sayin' he ain't yours?"

"Stupid tramp!" I tossed in the wind. "This broad really got a baby by you?" Suddenly, I felt like my son had been reduced to nothing. He wasn't the oldest, he wasn't the youngest, he wasn't even the one by the baby mama his daddy loved. He was just one of Quamir's kids. "You ain't nothing, Quamir! Matter of fact, it doesn't even matter what you do 'cause I'm out!"

"And I'm done with you, too," Shanice said. "I'm sick of you cheating on me!"

"Hos is always schemin'," Quamir said. "Man, please. Both y'all knew the deal and now you tryna act like you ain't know about the other? Now if you wanna stomp each other, then don't talk about it, be about it!" He stepped from in front of me. "What I care!"

Shanice started going off on Quamir, but I stood there. Stunned. Embarrassed. Wishing I could fly away and nobody would see me. Although he hadn't hit me, I felt like I'd been beaten. Why would he play me like this? What happened to him falling on his knees and telling this chick I was wifey?

I became anxious and didn't know what to do, where to turn, or how to act. I thought about crying but couldn't get any tears to come out. Then I thought about dying, but thinking of my son reminded me I had a reason to live. Then it hit me, I felt like nothing, as if all my wind had been sucked out and all that was left was a worthless shell.

"I'm leaving," Seven spat. "If you wanna stay here and take this crap, then do you, but me, I'm outta here!"

I stood there for a moment before walking backward to the car and getting in. I knew I looked crazy; I felt out of my mind. As the three of us got in the car and slammed the doors, I tried my best to believe what I was about to say. "I am so done with his ass!" I sniffed as tears covered my cheeks like glaze. "And I know he gon' come back beggin' me . . . like he always does. But I promise you, he gon' have to work real hard to get back with me. 'Cause I'm not beat for this no more!"

"You sound," Seven said, shaking her head as we drove off, "so damn dumb."

HAVEN'T HAD ENOUGH?
CHECK OUT THESE OTHER GREAT SERIES
FROM DAFINA BOOKS!

DRAMA HIGH

by L. Divine

Follow the adventures of a young sistah who's learning life in the 'hood is nothing compared to life in high school.

THE FIGHT
ISBN: 0-7582-1633-5

SECOND CHANCE
ISBN: 0-7582-1635-1

AYD'S LEGACY
ISBN: 0-7582-1637-8

FRENEMIES
ISBN: 0-7582-2532-6

LADY J
ISBN: 0-7582-2534-2

BOY SHOPPING

by Nia Stephens

An exciting "you pick the ending" series that lets the reader pick Mr. Right.

BOY SHOPPING
ISBN: 0-7582-1929-6

LIKE THIS AND LIKE THAT
ISBN: 0-7582-1931-8

GET MORE
ISBN:0-7582-1933-4

DEL RIO BAY

by Paula Chase

A wickedly funny series that explores friendship, betrayal, and how far some people will go for popularity.

SO NOT THE DRAMA
ISBN: 0-7582-1859-1

DON'T GET IT TWISTED
ISBN: 0-7582-1861-3

PERRY SKKY JR.

by Stephanie Perry Moore

An inspirational series that follows the adventures of a high school football star as he balances faith and the temptations of teen life.

PRIME CHOICE
ISBN: 0-7582-1863-X

PRESSING HARD
ISBN: 0-7582-1872-9

PROBLEM SOLVED
SBN: 0-7582-1874-5

PRAYED UP
ISBN: 0-7582-2538-5